If I Met You First...

M/M Enemies to Lovers Romance

.

By

.

A.B Julian

The Right One Series: Vol 1. ed 2

Published by A.B Julian Books, Inc,

2023

Table of Contents

This book is dedicated to my beautiful sister.

If I Met You First...

A.B Julian

COPYRIGHT

4

Synopsis

Xander

.

Never fall for an enemy, especially when he is your best friend's ex. Out of all people, Myles Alden is not the mistake you want to make. The man has a God complex; you would think he'd have tamed after being dumped in front of all our friends. But no, of course not. Myles Alden is full of himself. And it is just my luck that he is my new boss.

.

Myles

.

Xander is not someone I can ever fall for, or that's what I tell myself. Xander is a self-righteous swindler who thinks he has a right to judge my every move when he is the one who has no ethics. After hating on me all this time, he dared apply for a contract with my company. Xander does not know what he signed up for. I will make his life hell.

Chapter One

This is how we met

.

Xander

.

"What kind of a ridiculous joke is this? Who let him in?" were the first few words Myles Alden uttered as soon as I entered his prestigious office and our eyes met.

Sitting behind that fancy office desk in that expensive tailor-made suit, at the boss chair, Myles Alden didn't even bother directly communicating with a pest like me.

He was enraged when he learned that his head office dared choose me as the new interior designer and event planner for his latest housing project.

"Has anyone even taken the time to review his portfolio before letting him in my office?" He asked his assistant, then he ordered her to get rid of me immediately and find someone more suitable for the job.

I couldn't entirely blame him. Scratch that, I could totally blame him, and it's my point of view anyway. The thing is, this wasn't the first time Myles and I were in a face-off, we had a history. *And no, not that kind of history, he's not my type.* Myles Alden was the ex-boyfriend of my best friend, Simon.

"Cathy, I am not looking to hire someone to throw a birthday party for my ninety-year-old grandma. I need a professional. It will be the first exhibition of our model home, and our goal is to sell all the houses before they even go to the market. This open house event is the key. We cannot hire someone whose best experience is organizing a baby shower," Myles scolded his assistant.

"Myles," I opened my mouth... and he stopped me,

"It's Mr. Alden, and I wasn't talking to you," at least he bothered to look at me directly.

I took a deep breath. I needed this, it was a once-in-a-lifetime opportunity for a designer like me. Let's face it. A pond fish would never be invited to swim in a shark-sized tank like Eldwine Industries. When I submitted the tender for other big names like Eldwine, I had no delusion of ever being selected. However, by some miracle, I was selected, which was way past the tender's closing date. This means the first choice that won the tender was now fired in the middle of the busy season, and I was here as a last resort for Eldwines. I was not stupid to let my ego get in the way of this opportunity that could set me up for life.

"Mr. Alden," I started again. "My agency has done more than just arrange grandma's birthday parties or baby showers. I have a team of experienced professionals that ..."

"Shut up, Xander," Myles cut me off, making it perfectly clear that he was nowhere interested in listening to anything I had to offer. So, I did shut up, and with sudden silence in the office, our eyes got locked into each other, and the first thing that ran through my idiot brain was that I forgot how green Myles' eyes were.

The last time our eyes met like this, Myles had said, and I quote, "You know Xander, the upside of this breakup with Simon is that I wouldn't have to ever see your face again."

I had then replied, "Of course, only a pompous, self-absorbed jerk like you can see an upside to being dumped since admitting that you deserved it would be too much for your ego."

At the time, I wasn't planning on ever seeing Myles again. But standing in Myles Alden's office right now, I realize why keeping your thoughts to yourself is considered wise.

"Alexander, why don't you give us a minute? I'll call you shortly," Cathy, his sweet assistant, walked me out of Myles' office to the waiting area.

◆◆◆◆◆

As I mentioned, it wasn't the first time I met Myles. We first met at Simon's apartment, which hadn't gone very well either. I'd hated him then, and I hate him now and believe me, it wasn't my fault the first time either. Myles had it in for me from the get-go.

"The best friend, of course. Simon mentions you in almost every conversation. Alex, right?" that's what Myles said the first time we met.

"Xander," I corrected him while I shook his strong, manicured hand.

"Huh?" he raised his eyebrows.

"Xander, short for Alexander, no one calls me Alex." There was no way in hell my best friend Simon would have ever introduced me as Alex to his boyfriend.

He smirked in response, "Of course, Xander, having multiple names can be difficult to remember. I'm Myles Alden, nothing for short," I knew right then that he was a prick, but I decided to give him the presumption of innocence for Simon's sake.

"Myles, is that a family name?" I was just making a conversation to ignore the 'multiple names' comment.

"Yes, I am named after my great-grandfather."

I just nodded in response. I had no intention of deepening the conversation.

"So, why were you named Alexander? What's so great about you?" okay, was that sarcastic? I couldn't tell at the time.

"I guess my Mom liked the name." I shrugged.

"Your parents didn't tell you?"

"No, my mom was too drunk and overdosed to tell me anything, and I know nothing about my father," I bluntly replied.

Myles gazed at me in response as if he found me worth exploring, and I had this strange déjà vu feeling like it wasn't the first time Myles looked at me like that. As if we had met before, which was impossible. Let's say it was not the type of feelings you want to have for your best friend's boyfriend.

"Myles, it's not Xander's favourite topic," Simon interrupted whatever moment we were having.

I silently thanked Simon as we sat at the dinner table. Then Myles had a little chitchat with the rest of our friends, Jenny, Micky and Tommy. They also had multiple names, one on the papers and another for us friends. But I didn't hear Myles comment anything rude to any of them. I was his one and only favourite because Myles again directed the conversation towards me.

"So, I hear you are an artist, Xander? Simon is very fond of your art."

I know, on the surface, there was nothing malice about what Myles said, but it was the way he said it like he took a pause before saying my name and the way he made it a question. On top of that, he gave me this look that made me feel like I had to prove my worth.

"Simon is probably my biggest and only fan," I smiled at Simon as we started unwrapping the takeout Chinese I brought.

"Not true. I have seen how boys at his college used to go gaga over the scale models he made," Simon was always so sweet, nothing like Myles or me.

"That's nice, so what do you do for a living, Xander?" See, I was correct. Myles Alden was a prick.

I felt like responding with, *'I'm an artist, dah,'* but I could see Simon's crimson cheeks from my peripheral vision and decided to avoid any rude comebacks.

"I'm an interior designer," I replied politely.

"Xander runs his own event planning business now," Simon added proudly. But I could tell his self-assured jerk of a boyfriend wasn't impressed.

"I see," he exhibited the perfect use of those chopsticks. "I deal with a lot of designers in my business. I don't recall ever hearing your name, Xander."

Here we go. if Myles Alden thought he could intimidate me, he was in for a big surprise. Myles wasn't the first rich asshole I was dealing with.

"Oh yeah? You mean the business you run for your Daddy?"

Simon choked on his noodles. I gave him a quick glance and blamed the chopstick he was using just to impress Myles.

"You are okay?" Myles handed Simon the glass of water like a perfect boyfriend.

"Yeah," Simon gulped the water down.

Then Myles gave me that smug smile as he looked me in the eyes, "Eldwine Custom Homes Builders, we are in the top ten list of the builders in the New York state." he gave that haughty smirk. I knew about Eldwine Industries, of course. Still, I squinted my eyes at him in question, "family business that I'm now taking over," he added proudly.

"Good for you. Your father must be proud," I smiled at him. "Ouch," I yelped because Simon had kicked me under the table, and we both glared at each other, but Myles was too busy bragging.

"Let's see, A. I've always been at the top of my class. B. According to the number one Builder Magazine, I'm among the most successful businessmen in the housing industry. C. Eldwine has been nominated twice for BRCH awards since I joined, that's Build Renovate Custom Homes Awards, one and the very best," he added, even though nobody asked, "so yes, my father is very proud."

There was this challenge in Myles' eyes, which irritated and intrigued me at the same time.

"A, B, C, huh? Who can argue with that?" I smiled and tried my best to leave the conversation at that.

I didn't have any Daddy's money to show for. These perfect frat boys like Myles Alden with Daddy's money were on the top of my list to avoid for a reason. The truth was I didn't belong anywhere near Myles Alden. The only reason an uptown guy like Simon and I were friends was that we used to be roommates. When Simon's family threw him out on the streets for being gay, he needed a home, and I needed someone to share my rent. So, we became roommates and then best friends. Later, Simon's parents accepted him, but Simon stayed with me until he bought this new fancy apartment with his new job as a family lawyer. He asked me to move in with him, but there was no way I could afford the rent to this place, and I wasn't taking any help from Simon. So, long story short, I was only sitting across a rich asshole like Myles at the same dinner table because of Simon.

I didn't belong in Myles Alden's world, and he was doing his best to remind me just that. He even offered me money for the food I bought for dinner, and mind you, we all bought something for dinner, just as the fancy wine Myles had brought. Still, Myles offered to pay only me, which I very graciously refused. Simon said Myles' intention was to help. He just didn't know how, but I could sense his sole purpose in offering to pay for the dinner I bought was to insult me. The only thing I didn't understand was why.

I left pretty soon after that. But again, it wasn't the only time I met Myles. Every time I did, he made sure to make me feel unwelcomed. And he wasn't just shitty to me, he was also shitty to Simon. Myles constantly reminded Simon that he should have taken property law just like his father if he wanted to be successful. I thought Simon was doing great for himself, after all, he bought this expensive apartment.

"Simon enjoys family law," I had spoken in defence of Simon, "it's his choice what he does. Also, he is good at it, right, Simon?"

"I wouldn't call it good," Simon smiled shyly.

It's like watching a train wreck, and the worst part of it was that Simon didn't even see it. He was too much in awe of his perfect, new, handsome boyfriend, Myles Alden. Oh yeah, he was handsome, alright. Just like those models in the business suit magazines, which were exclusively available at custom tailor's shops. Speaking of which, I bet he didn't buy his clothes at any store like the rest of us commoners, he got them custom-made, and he looked damn good in it. *Ignoring that.*

I still tried to encourage the low-esteemed Simon.

"Of course you are good. Last week, you told me about a client whose husband wasn't paying child support. What happened to that case?" I asked.

"Oh yeah, the father claimed he was broke and couldn't pay child support. The court ordered him to have half of his paycheck directly deposited to the mother of his children's account every week."

"Wow, now that's something," I smiled and met Myles' eyes with a challenge.

"Only, the mother wasn't my client. The father was." Simon shrugged, and Myles acted like he could barely hold his laugh.

"That was just one case. Simon has won cases before, right, Simon?"

"Yeah," Simon started to say, but his pompous ass boyfriend interrupted.

"I'm not saying there is no money in family law if you actually have clients that are not broke," he shrugged. It was true Simon didn't have wealthy clients, but it didn't mean he was a lousy lawyer and couldn't make it big. "It just takes a special skill to get those clients," Myles added, taking a satisfactory sip from his glass as he met my eyes.

So, this is how we met.

Chapter Two

No, this is how we met

.

Myles

.

Every time I'd set my eyes on Xander, I felt that he was sent on this earth, mainly to exasperate me.

Contrary to the popular notion, it wasn't my first time meeting Xander. No, not in my office right now or the first time Simon, my ex, introduced me to his best friend Xander at his apartment.

"Alex" that's the name he gave me the first time we met.

It was the graduation night, we were all in high spirits. I hadn't yet come out to everyone but a few friends. Alan, one of my friends, had told me he knew a club on the other side of the town that could probably get me what I wanted. Going to another side of the town was like crossing a border for upper-class kids like us. But then there was this promise of a real party on the other side of the city with drugs, guns and sex. I wasn't really eager about the guns and drugs, but sex, hell yeah. And that's what the rest of the guys said when we jumped into Alan's jeep that drove us straight out of town to the club where no one knew us, and we could be whoever we wanted to be without having to worry about the high stakes of our surnames.

The club was near the harbour. It looked like any other club on the surface. The things I noticed that distinguished it from other clubs were that it required a unique password for entry, it stunk of weed, and the bartender didn't even card us before handing us our drinks, even though I was pretty sure my friend Jason looked barely eighteen. All that aside, the best thing was the feeling of freedom in the air.

The music was excellent. Everyone was moving with the beat. Many hot guys and girls were on the floor, swaying with rhythm, showing off their bodies, but there was this one guy who kept catching my attention. He was dancing with another man. He had that beautiful brownish blond hair, golden tan and perfect slim physique of a runway model. I only got a glimpse of his face a few times when he turned in my direction. I tried to look at other men since I could see he was with someone else.

My eyes kept going back to him. He was just moving with the other man on the dance floor as if dancing was a chore. They were not touching each other, just dancing with the beat. I looked around, and a few girls and guys nodded at me with interest, but I found myself looking at the same guy again. I was admiring his body again when the man he was dancing with leaned forward, and I thought he was going to kiss him. I probably wouldn't mind watching, but I was wary of the place and being called on it, yet I couldn't look away. They didn't kiss, though. Instead, the other guy whispered something in his ear, and at that exact moment, he turned to look straight at me. When his golden hazel eyes met mine, I knew I wasn't as subtle as I was trying to be, and I almost dropped my beer. The guy was beautiful, and I was done when he checked me out from top to bottom. But then he turned back to his dancing partner and whispered something in his ear. I tried looking away. I was in no way looking for a fight. The idea was to quietly get in, have fun and get out.

To my surprise, that beautiful guy started walking towards me, and I couldn't take my eyes off him. I had never seen a more stunning man than him. He was totally my type, and the type I didn't even know existed.

He stood next to me and leaned in to speak over the music, "Buy me a drink," his breath on my ear sent goosebumps through my skin.

"Sure," I smiled. I was young, and the guy was younger than me, but I probably looked like an idiot as I tried to catch the bartender's attention. "Excuse me," I kept calling the bartender, but he wouldn't listen to me, which was embarrassing. If Alan hadn't bought me my beer, I'd have to stay thirsty.

"Hey Maxie," the pretty guy next to me, whom I was dying to impress, shouted and whistled to the bartender, whose name happened to be Maxie. Maxie turned with full attention to him, "Tell him what you want," the pretty guy reminded me to order. I ordered the mojito and a beer. The bartender looked me up before handing us our drinks. I quickly handed a twenty and didn't ask for change.

"Long way from home?" he asked, taking a sip from his drink, and my eyes zeroed on his lips like a perv.

"Is it that obvious?"

"You are too clean, and we don't get frat boys here," I was in a fraternity. It surprised me how observant he was as it looked like he barely paid any attention to me.

"What's your name?" I asked.

"Why do you need my name?" he turned to face me.

"I need to call you something," I tried speaking over the loud music.

"Okay, frat boy, for your future fantasies, you can call me Alex," he winked.

Alex, yeah, that's the name he gave me.

He downed his drink in one go.

"Come on, let's dance," he didn't precisely ask, he just grabbed my hand and pulled me to the dance floor.

Knowing I was terrible at dancing, I was about to object when he spooned his body into mine, and my inexperienced mind blew away. He grabbed my arm and wrapped it around himself as he moved with slow, torturous speed against me. He smiled, knowing very well what he was doing to me. He pushed his hips against my groin, and I could barely move.

"You are not dancing," he whispered with that warm breath in my ear.

"I'm trying," I said and hated how my breath caught. He sniggered in response and turned.

"Are you out?" he whispered again.

I nodded, "recently."

"Am I your first?" he held my gaze in question.

"No," I lied.

"Why are you nervous then?" he moved closer again, putting his leg between mine. It took me some time to gather myself to answer him.

"I'd just never been with a stranger," what I meant to say, I had never been with a man, let alone a stranger from the other side of the town. It was exciting and scaring me. And now I was daydreaming. Alex was probably not interested in anything more than a dance.

He smiled and grabbed my hand, "Come on."

I followed him off the dance floor to the club's corner and then out the backdoor exit that read, 'staff only.'

Once outside, he pushed me to the wall and pressed his hot mouth to mine. I pulled him closer and kissed him senseless. His body felt so good in my arms. I wanted to kiss him more when he pulled back, then he smiled and used his two fingers to get something out of his pocket. For a second, I thought or hoped it was a condom, but when he pulled the wrapper, I saw it was an orange pill. He offered it to me.

"No, thanks," I refused.

He looked genuinely surprised, "are you sure?"

"Yeah, I don't do drugs," I realized this was the drugs part of this side of town. Not that we didn't have drugs on our side of the city. It just wasn't this easy. We had to plan, find a dealer, and be discreet about it.

"No? Not even steroids, Fratboy?" he pressed his hand against my chest and traced my muscles.

I shook my head, "No, not even steroids," he smiled in response, and his smile was gorgeous, and even that act when he placed that pill in his mouth and swallowed it was the sexiest thing I had ever seen. Then he moved forward and kissed me again, I could taste the orange, with that sweet taste of his, and I wasn't complaining when his lips moved down my throat. And his hands unbuckled my belt.

"You want me?" he asked.

"Yeah, I want you," I could barely stand. I couldn't remember if I had ever been this horny.

He brought his mouth closer to mine, and I thought he was going to give me that hot taste of his mouth again, but he said, "Then pay up."

"What?" I thought I heard it wrong.

"Two hundred," he said.

"Two hundred?"

"Now, don't act like it's big money to you, Fratboy. Pay up."

"I don't pay for sex," I said firmly.

He laughed in response. "Are you sure about that," he moved closer and slid his hand under my pants.

"Oh fuck," I could literally see stars.

"Now, come on, be a good Fratboy and pay up." he insisted.

"You are doing this for money?" I asked.

"You know how they say, when you are good at something, don't do it for free," he gave me that sexy smile that promised a lot.

"I'm pretty sure that's not what they meant. Oh fuck," I could barely stand when he used his hands to win the argument.

"You want me to stop, Fratboy?" he brought his sensual mouth closer to me again. I grabbed his arms, held him in place and kissed him hard. When I let go of him, I could see his dilated pupils. Maybe it was drugs, or perhaps he wanted me just as much as I wanted him.

So, I did what I had to. I took out my wallet and paid him two hundred. He gracefully placed the money in his back pocket and smiled.

On cue, a tattooed guy showed up, "Xander," oh yeah, that's what he had called him.

"Oh shit," Alex or Xander said.

"Hey, what are you doing with my boyfriend?" the tattooed man asked me. I was sure I would get beat up when two other men joined the angry tattooed guy.

But Xander stopped them, "Don't hit him, guys. He'll pay up for his mistake, won't you, Fratboy?" he winked.

So, this is how we met.

I was sure surprised to learn that Simon had a friend named Xander. It had been eight years since I met him that first time. I wanted to believe it wasn't the same Xander, but when I met him again at Simon's place and looked into those hazel eyes, I had no doubt it was him. Xander, however, had no such memory.

Xander

So, since the day we met, it had become my mission to pinpoint every single prick move Myles made. After all, it was my responsibility as a best friend to tell Simon how much of an asshole his boyfriend was. But Simon wasn't interested in listening. He was too busy turning into Myles' little puppet.

"I thought you didn't like coffee flavour in ice cream," I said to Simon when I opened his fridge to self-serve a bowl of ice cream and was surprised to see that there was no chocolate flavour, which Simon loved. And there was this healthy organic shit that Simon had zero taste for.

"I kind of like it now. It's not bad," he smiled, avoiding my eyes, "and I need to cut down on chocolate anyway. It's not healthy," he shrugged.

"And coffee is healthy?" I questioned, meeting his eyes. "Is that what Myles thinks?"

"It's not like that." was Simon's typical answer for everything. "If I don't like coffee, I'll eat less ice cream and stay healthy."

Seriously, that was the logic Simon gave me.

But these sudden changes in Simon's likes and dislikes were not limited to his food preferences. For example, he made excuses for every activity I suggested.

"Let's go to the movies," I said, and Simon's response was "excuses".

"Let's go to the gay bar," I asked.

Simon replied with, "Excuses."

"Let's go play community volleyball," I suggested.

Simon replied with, "Excuses."

And whenever I pointed out, "Did Myles say no?" "Did Myles say gay bars are lame?" Did Myles say theatres are for plays, not movies?" "Did Myles say the country club is much better than the community centre?"

"It's not like that," was Simon's answer to everything, so I stopped asking.

I hardly met Myles after that. We only met when all of our friends were hanging out, and he was there because he was invited, but he was usually too busy on his phone, working. Apparently, to him, only he had an important job.

The worst part was that being with Myles, Simon had started believing he was no good. He started thinking he only had a law degree because his father was one of the law school's chair members. This may be true to some extent. Simon may have gotten admission into law school because of his dad, but he sure as hell passed the school and the bar on his own merit. It was a significant achievement that somewhere got lost in Myles Alden's definition of a good lawyer.

"Why do you always have to compromise? Isn't he in a relationship too?" I was giving my piece of mind to Simon for cancelling on me for the third time. Apparently, the date to help at the charity event my agency was organizing conveniently crashed with Myles' plans to take Simon out for dinner with his client.

"Would it kill Myles to be considerate towards your needs once in a while?" I added.

"Xander, anytime you learn to shut up and decide to mind your own fucking business, be sure to let me know," It wasn't sweet Simon who replied. Of course, it was the asshole boyfriend, Myles Alden.

I was bitching about Myles out loud because I thought Simon and I were alone in his apartment, but of course not. Myles came out of Simon's bedroom and stood behind me. He obviously heard everything I had said about him and Simon's relationship. I could literally feel the fire coming out of my head. I told myself I didn't care if Myles heard me and turned to face my adversary, who was in an unbuttoned shirt. I tried not to look at his abs, I only cared about Simon. He was my best friend, and whatever I said was in his best interest.

"Myles, Xander doesn't mean anything by it," Simon was giving justification on my behalf instead of agreeing with me. He clearly was in Myles' corner.

"Of course, he doesn't. Besides, we don't need relationship advice from someone who never had a stable relationship," Myles smirked, holding my gaze with a challenge.

"I had plenty of relationships," okay, that was a stupid response.

"Plenty, I'm sure." He smirked. "But plenty doesn't mean stable. And going back to the same person, after being cheated on so many times, isn't very smart either."

Our eyes had locked into each other for a few painful seconds until Simon spoke, "Myles."

"Not that I care for your thoughts, but thank you very much for pointing it out," I retorted.

"You are most welcome," he smiled.

I glared at him and turned to leave.

"Xander, listen," Simon called after me, following me to the door. "Please don't go like this. I didn't say anything to Myles about you and Ryan. It's just that when you didn't show up for commingling night this month, everyone was talking about you and Ryan out of concern," Simon pleaded.

"I know, it's not your fault," I hugged Simon. It's not like it was a secret. All my friends knew, and I wasn't proud that I had gone back to Ryan, my ex, more times than I'd like to count. Myles was right about one thing. I was in no place to give Simon any relationship advice when I wasn't setting the best example.

"And, I'm sorry, I shouldn't have ditched you last minute," Simon apologized again.

"Don't worry, I'll find someone. It won't be as good as you, but will do. I'll call you tomorrow." I kissed Simon on the forehead before I left. Simon was so sweet, and Myles was such a douche.

Chapter Three

You think you know me

·

Myles

·

So, I was the douche. That's what Xander told my ex-boyfriend Simon. Our relationship may have ended because Simon cheated on me, but one of the reasons for it was Xander. Instead of feeling guilty for cheating on me, Simon said I asked for it because I didn't treat him right, and there was no way Simon came up with that conclusion alone. I could literally see Xander's fingerprints all over Simon's plan to dump me in such a humiliating fashion. Simon organized this get-together with all his friends to tell me he was leaving me since I was a prick and didn't treat him right. The thing was, Simon was way too sweet to use those words with me, but Xander lived to make me livid.

·

Xander

·

Myles lived to make me livid. His unwarranted comments fell like a bomb with the perfect aim to my head, for instance, the time he said, and I quote, "It always helps to have wealthy friends around. Anytime you need money, they work like ATMs."

It was one fucking time when I forgot my wallet at home and asked to borrow money from Simon to pay for the cab. I know I should have called Uber now that I think. The point is I paid back to Simon right there with my phone. But no, Mr. I Am So Perfect, had to comment and make me feel cheap.

And it wasn't just that one time. There was another one, "Free food is always good, isn't it, Xander?"

Or my favourite, "Maybe you can pay for dinner next time, Xander. I bet you have extra cash now from the rent you are collecting on your apartment since you are living here for free."

I wasn't living at Simon's apartment for free. Simon had a terrible skiing accident, and Myles was too busy to take care of him, so I had to stay with Simon, walk him to the bathroom, and help him dress. Either Myles was too ignorant to see all that, or he chose to be an asshole.

I couldn't understand how Simon could live with Myles. He couldn't possibly be that good in bed.

Myles

Xander judged me every day of my relationship with Simon when he was the kind of person who couldn't even remember who he was in bed with last night.

Xander

Sure, I wasn't perfect. I did things and said some things that I shouldn't have. I still regretted telling Myles that he deserved to be cheated on. Not my finest hour. No matter how much of an asshole Myles had been to me, no one deserved to be cheated on.

Myles

"Simon doesn't feel sorry because maybe you deserve to be cheated on," were the kind words Alexander Rossi had showered me with the last time I saw him.

I swore to myself that day that instead of crying over my breakup with Simon, I'd cherish this day because I wouldn't have to see Xander's face again. Nonetheless, here we were again. I couldn't believe he dared submit a tender with Eldwine Industries when he hated me so much.

.

Xander

.

As I was told, I waited outside Myles' office. I had no hope of getting this contract anymore. I don't know why I thought I wouldn't have to deal with Myles Alden at his own business. Why on earth would he accept my business proposal when he hated me so much?

Surprisingly, I was called into Myles' office again and offered a chair this time.

There was no attitude change in Myles Alden, though, so I was probably invited in to be insulted some more. That's what I thought until Cathy told me that I got the contract as I was promised, but I had to prove myself. So, while I worked on the main project, I'd also have to arrange a minor event first.

I didn't mind organizing a smaller event as long as I got paid. I was very confident in my abilities until Myles added, "And if you fail at that minor event, you'd be immediately terminated, and you'll have to pay the penalty for wasting our precious time."

My mouth suddenly felt dry, "How much penalty?"

"Payback the deposit, of course, and half of what your company is worth." He paused to look me in the eyes. "Do you accept Mr. Rossi?" he added.

I was so furious I had no words. I just stared at Myles, and he smirked at me, and then I realized he was so sure I would turn this offer down. And he was counting on it, which meant he didn't have the power to terminate my verbal agreement with their marketing director at their head office.

It was a big gamble, but now I wasn't backing down. Mr. Almighty Perfect didn't have the power to reject me. Now, this I had to see through.

"I accept," as soon as the words came out of my mouth, I watched intently how his smirk changed into shock and then rage.

"Fine, let's put it on papers, Cathy," Myles said, restoring back to the factory setting of the smug face he always had.

"Thank you, Mr. Alden," I said as I stood to shake his hand, which he ignored and sniggered in response.

"Don't thank me yet, Xander. You don't know what you signed up for." His piercing green eyes told me I was so fucked.

"This way, Mr. Rossi," Cathy said, and I followed.

"Oh Cathy, also tell Mr. Rossi about our dress code."

"Ah, sure," Cathy flushed, looking embarrassed.

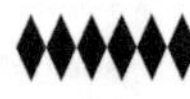

Myles

I'd rather deal with Xander than talk to my father about getting rid of Xander. Besides, all I had to do was watch Xander fail. How hard could that be? Xander had no idea what he said yes to. I was going to make his life hell.

Xander

Season's first snow felt so good on my skin. This year was supposed to be less snow, but weather journalists never got it right. I knocked at the door of Mrs. Cook's group home for boys, where I was once a resident and now was here to pay my due diligence.

"You are early, Xander," Mrs. Cook said as she opened the door.

"Yeah, I brought you all some breakfast," I brought the packages inside and kept them on the kitchen counter. It was still early, so all the boys were asleep.

"Oh, you are a God-sent, Xander. It smells delicious. All the boys would appreciate something nice for a change," she peeked in the bags and added, "Xander, this looks like it cost you."

"I got this new project for big builders. They paid me big advance," I smiled.

"Congratulations, I am proud of you," she hugged me.

"Thanks. I just came to say I'd be busy for a while, but I'll come back for the holidays,"

"Good for you. Of course, boys will miss your cooking skills, but it would be a good drill for them to be independent. And I am very happy for you and proud," she hugged me again. She was my only real family. If I got a big contract, I had to share it with her because I knew she'd be genuinely happy for me. "So, you found your Mr. Right yet?" my thoughts involuntarily went to Myles for no reason, and I shook my head.

"Why do you always ask me that?"

"Just so you don't lose hope, it's very easy to lose hope in the busy world," she smiled kindly.

I sighed, nodded with a smile and busied myself serving breakfast for the boys. I didn't admit to Mrs. Cook that I lost hope long ago. I wasn't a teen anymore, and there was no Mr. Right.

"So, tell me about the new project," she asked.

"The project is great. I actually got three jobs in total, two events and one interior designing project. It's just perfect except..."

"Except?"

"The boss doesn't like me, and that's putting it mildly."

"Oh, my boy, he must be blind then or old and ugly,"

"No, he is very nice-looking. He's, in fact, one of the best-looking men I've ever seen, and he's smart. He's got this fancy degree, but not just because of his degree. He's very spontaneous, and this thing about him ..." I stopped myself from praising Myles Alden any more than I already had. I could feel the tip of my ears being red the way Mrs. Cook watched me. "I just need you to pray for me, Mrs. Cook," I said.

"I always pray for you, but this one I sure will light a candle for," she winked with a smile.

Chapter Four

I do know you

.

Myles

.

I watched Xander through the glass door of my office. He was climbing two steps at a time. Xander looked more cheery than when he was in my office the day before. I watched that effortless smile on his lips while he talked to Cathy. I focused a bit longer on his well-formed, slender body in those skin-hugging jeans and that sexy dress shirt than I liked to admit. I wanted to ignore him, but the problem with Xander was that it was impossible to ignore him. Then maybe I didn't have to this time. After all, my goal was to kick Xander out of my life forever, and that task required giving Xander my full attention.

.

Xander

.

"So, when do I get to see the site?" I asked Cathy while she was messaging I.T. to hurry up on my access.

"You don't," it wasn't Cathy who answered my question. It was that arrogant prick, Myles. You could just hear the arrogance in his voice, "You'll work with the blueprints." He told me, "Cathy will give you access," he added.

"Working on it," Cathy replied.

"Blueprints are okay, but I thought I'd visit the site too to get a better visual," I told Myles.

"Why? Don't you know how to read the blueprints or visualize them? What about that Industrial Designer degree you have? Is it even real?"

"It's real, and my major was Interior Design, but that's not the point. I need to see the house to get more inspiration."

"Inspiration," he scoffed, "of course, because you are an artist." It wasn't an acknowledgement but sarcasm, "The site isn't ready. If your artistic inspiration needs visuals, work with the scale model. You can check out the work our previous designer has done on the project so far and take it from there."

I opened my mouth to object that I couldn't just take other designer's work, but Cathy interrupted.

"I.T. will get you your laptop and tablet, you can work from your office, and James will get you the detailed blueprints," Cathy informed.

Thinking about working in an office's closed environment already started to give me a headache. I thought I could take the laptop and work from somewhere else.

It's like Myles read my mind and said, "One more thing, those prints are not out for the public - they securely stay on the Eldwine server. You cannot take those blueprints off Eldwine premises. Understood?" he asked.

"Yes, Boss," I concurred, and Myles glared at me, then returned to his perfect smirk.

"Good. I didn't hear your concern about your first project. You do remember that you only get to work on the housing project if you complete the first challenge," Myles eyed me.

"It's not much of a challenge. I'm not just an expert in baby shower and grandma's birthday parties, you know," I smiled.

Myles gave me one of his best smirks, which distracted me enough to pause a little.

"Wedding anniversary is, in fact, my agency's specialty, and nothing brings me more joy than helping married couples cherish their love for each other. So, this challenge of yours is a piece of cake for me," I smiled confidently, but he laughed in response.

"See, this is where you are wrong, Xander. It's my parent's thirtieth anniversary, and my parents are no ordinary couple. They don't want to throw this anniversary party to cherish their love for each other. Hell, I'd be surprised if they even like each other. They only tolerate one another because they have a status to uphold. And that's where you come in. You have to maintain that status. It's an event to market the perfect image of a happy couple, not a get-together party for personal pleasure. And just so you know, my father would decide if you completed the challenge. He is a very picky man. Meeting his expectations is not a piece of cake, and if he's not impressed, you are out of the contract," I had started recognizing the little glitter Myles got in his eyes when he was up to something, that never ended well for me.

"In that case, I should get a start on the anniversary first," I said to Cathy.

"Wise choice. You only have four days to arrange this world-class party," Myles threw another bomb at my head.

"Four days? I thought you said it's next week?" I looked at Cathy for confirmation.

"It is next week," Cathy got up on her feet.

"Weather is really nice this week, isn't it, Cathy?"

"It is," she responded gradually.

"Yes, that's why I moved the date to this Saturday, so you have exactly four days to prepare for this event," Myles smirked.

"Four days? That's not enough time," I said desperately.

"You already sound like you are ready to fold, Xander," Myles remarked.

"Not in a million years, Myles!" I countered.

"Call me, Boss. I liked the sound of it," Locking his eyes with mine, he said a little close to my face.

"I'm not here to satisfy your narcissistic, kinky side, Myles." I stepped back to walk away when he quickly blocked my way.

"If I were you, Xander, I'd worry more about not getting on my wrong side," he threatened.

"I'll keep that in mind, Boss," I glared at him, but he smiled with that spark in his eyes.

The visit to Myles' parents' mansion

After waiting half an hour, I was allowed into the mansion to meet Mrs. Alden's assistant. She showed me around, it was a big mansion.

"I'd need to meet Mr. and Mrs. Alden to see what they are looking for?" I requested but was told to watch the last anniversary's video and get inspiration there.

I watched the video, which was a total waste of my time. Last year's anniversary had no personal touch. It was just an expensive party.

Later, I got the pleasure of meeting Mr. Edwin Alden, Myles' father. I'm not sure if I should call it a pleasure, though. I noticed Myles inherited his good looks and arrogance from this man.

"Myles told me you would be handling our anniversary this year," Mr. Alden said while he was busy choosing the matching watch with his suit. Why would someone need so many expensive watches? I wore just one watch my entire life, and it worked fine. "It's a shame we had to let go of our previous event planner, even though she was the best," Mr. Alden continued, and I didn't interrupt. "We usually hire the best of class. Even our interns are graduates from top Universities. I don't suppose you could afford better schooling," ouch, "so don't feel pressured, boy, no one is expecting much out of you anyway." He smiled as he kindly thumped my shoulder with that very hand that now wore one of the most expensive watches I'd ever seen.

I'm still perplexed if Mr. Alden was trying to reassure or insult me, but one thing could not be more transparent: he was indeed Myles Alden's father. Mr. Edwin Alden sure knew how to belittle people with kind words.

Later, Mrs. Alden's chatty assistant, Ruby, informed me that the previous event planner was let go because she was too cozy with Mr. Alden. So, now Mr. Alden was under strict instructions by Mrs. Alden to never hire a female event planner again. So, here I was. I obviously didn't meet Mr. Alden's standards, but apparently, my manhood got me this job. Also, the fact that this time of year was booked in advance for other planners, the ones that apparently went to the best Art Schools in the country, which I could never afford. This whole revelation answered my other question, though. Myles couldn't fire me because it was his father who had hired me, and apparently, he couldn't overrule his father.

.

Since Mrs. Alden had refused to see me, I had to rely on the chatty Ruby. I was grateful she was so talkative. She told me almost everything I needed to know to prepare for the party. Where and how did Mr. and Mrs. Alden meet? The year they met. How many children? I had already set up a meeting with Myles' elder sister, Sophie. Unlike the rest of the Alden family, Sophie sounded warm and welcoming on the phone. And since I couldn't meet Mrs. Alden, her daughter was my best bet. Now, the only thing standing in my way was Mr. and Mrs. Alden's feelings for each other. If Mr. Alden had recently cheated on Mrs. Alden, no amount of decoration would bring any pleasure for either of them. But I had to try.

I may have not only thrown the baby showers, which Myles enjoyed reminding me of, but Alden mansion was the most extensive site I was getting the opportunity to work with. Okay the last thing I needed was Myles Alden to get into my head.

The site was huge, but so was the budget. I had never been allowed such a budget. I could do wonders.

I started making notes for the caterers. And then I was going to visit Mrs. Alden's friends.

◆◆◆◆◆

Myles stormed into my office without a knock, throwing a transaction sheet in front of me, "Did you order a bunch of expensive costumes for my parents' anniversary?" he asked.

"Yes, this is correct. I did," I confirmed, glancing at the transaction and amount.

"Let me guess, Xander, you are inviting drag queens off the street to my parents' anniversary?" he sat in front of me.

"Not this time, but if I'd have to throw a party for you, drag queens would be on the top of my list," we glared at each other for a few beats until he smirked again.

"Won't that be easy for you? I bet that's how you make extra bucks since you suck at event planning," he had that spark in his eyes again. *Don't let him get under your skin,* I reminded myself.

"Costumes are part of the theme for the party. Is that all you wanted to know, or is there anything else I can do for you, Myles?"

"Call me Boss," he said softly with a smile.

"I didn't hear anyone else call you boss around here," I argued.

"I'm not talking about others. I want you to call me Boss, Xander," he smirked.

"Is that so? Something special about me, Myles?" I smiled and batted my eyes.

For a few seconds, he just smirked and checked me out from top to bottom, making me a smidge of uncomfortable. Then he stood up straight and walked around the table. He grabbed the back of my chair and moved it so I'd face him. Then he bent a little to bring his face closer to mine, making my heart race at full speed.

"Let's see, your eyes have nice shades of green and yellow, complimenting your hair. Your eyes are a nice shape too, the eyelashes look almost real." My eyelashes were real, but as soon as I opened my mouth to tell him, he brought his mouth closer to mine. My heart skipped a beat, "your nose is not so big, your lips are ... I'd give it a six. Maybe attractive to someone who's into flowers. Your height is alright, your body is... " he closely checked me out, making my body to heat up, "a bit too slender for my taste." Then he met my eyes again, "So, no, there's nothing special about you. You are not my type, Xander." He smirked and pulled away from me while I sat there burning which I wanted to believe was because I was infuriated.

"Hey you," I finally recovered enough to stand up, but I didn't know what I was going to say when he interrupted me anyway.

"Boss, I said, call me Boss, and by the way, I cancelled the caterer," he added.

"Caterer?" It took me some time to get back to reality. "But why? It was the same caterer last year, and everyone loved their food."

"Exactly my point, that was the caterer from last year. You don't get to take anything from last year, Xander. You like to prove yourself. Arrange everything yourself."

"But we only have two days," I said. How would I find a caterer to replace the best caterer in the city in two days?

"Exactly. Get to work, Xander," he smiled proudly and left, shutting the door behind him.

"Son of a bitch," I opened the computer and started checking the list of caterers.

Chapter Five

You are playing with fire

·

Xander

·

T*he Night of The Wedding Anniversary*

·

It was the event night, I still didn't have the privilege to meet Mrs. Alden yet, and everything I had planned depended on Mrs. Alden's cooperation. Why did I even think my planning would be enough to impress her and join me? Maybe Myles was right, this couple didn't care about reliving their memories. All they cared about was their status in society.

Don't let Myles Alden bring you down, I reminded myself once again.

"Hmm, this is really good. You should try some, Xander," Ruby chimed. Everything smelled good, and the snacks were delicious. Glen, my friend and assistant, had tasted each item. At least the caterers I hired from the south of the town were doing a tremendous job.

"Thanks, guys, you've done a great job at such short notice," I told the caterers.

"You are kidding? We should thank you, Xander. We could never even dream of getting such a big contract. We are all set for a year," Tony, the head of the caterers, said.

"That's great. Just make sure everyone wears uniform, keep clean, wear gloves, and don't chit chat with the guests. If any guest doesn't like anything, do not argue with them, say sorry, offer them a replacement, if they don't take it, apologies again and immediately get out of their face, got it?" I instructed.

"You've got it, Boss," Tony said and added, "You've all heard the man," he said to his team, and they also gave me a thumbs up.

The word 'boss, reminded me of Myles. But I didn't have time to delve into it.

"The band is not showing up," Eric, the assistant I hired to assist Glen, informed. Apparently, the band cancelled at the last minute.

"You can't cancel at the last minute! You would have to turn in the deposit and pay the penalty." I warned the music band leader on the phone.

"I already did," the band leader said and hung up on me.

"What?" I tried calling him repeatedly, but the asshole didn't answer my phone.

"See, I told you, they are so rude," Eric looked like he was going to cry.

"Was that the musician?" Myles asked, "Cancelling last minute? How unprofessional. Right, Xander?" Myles grinned at me. Glen took Eric with him.

"Myles, you did this?" I asked, holding his gaze, and for a second, I felt he was sorry, but then he resumed back to his smug self.

"You bet I did. You didn't think I'd let you have this easy, Xander. This is war, after all," it sounded more like an explanation than a challenge.

"I didn't think you'd be so hell-bound on winning over me that you will destroy your parent's thirtieth anniversary," I was about to lose it. I was showing emotions to an enemy.

"Maybe this is your problem. If you knew me, you'd know that Myles Alden would do anything to win. But you don't really know me, Xander, do you?" He contended.

"Or maybe I know you too well, and that's what bothers you the most," I held his gaze in challenge.

"Is that so, Xander?" he defied, but he didn't seem so confident.

"You know what I think, Myles? This isn't about me. You are doing this to retaliate against your parents," I declared.

"Oh really, how so?" He tried to keep the facade, but I saw right through him.

"See, you have this calm exterior, but inside, you are so wounded about the fact that your father cheated on your mother, and your mother didn't do anything about it. And since you can't do anything about that, you are taking your frustration out on me." I stated.

He briefly stilled, and I knew I hit the bull's eye. After a second, he resorted back to his smug smile.

"If you are stupid enough to believe this is the first time my father cheated on my mother or the first time my mother found out, you are an idealist idiot, Xander, and definitely not cut out for this kind of business. This anniversary means nothing to me or my parents more than an opportunity to show off our wealth and maintain our status in the world of business," he paused and stepped closer as he added, "So, stop analyzing me because you didn't understand me when I was with Simon. And hell, you do not know me now. So, focus on your job. Without music, this party will be extremely boring." With that, he walked away. And I had little time to rummage into what this was about.

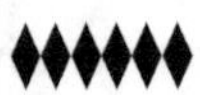

My phone rang, and I hoped it was Tony, the band leader, but it was Mrs. Cook.

God, I couldn't take any more bad news today. I worried as I answered the call.

"Hi, Mrs. Cook, everything alright?" I asked.

"Oh, yes, you told me you have your first event today. I am calling to wish you luck," I could hear the smile in her voice. "Xander?"

"Yeah, I hear you. Thank you."

"You don't sound alright, Xander," the concern in her voice touched me.

"Yeah," I couldn't believe I was about to cry. I felt like I was ten years old again, the time I had cried in front of Mrs. Cook for the first time, and she had hugged me. "My band quit on me last minute. I failed."

"Oh, sweetie, you didn't fail, don't give up."

"I'm not giving up, Mrs. Cook. I just don't know what to do?"

"Well, lucky for you, I know what to do," she said with so much confidence that it made me smile again.

.

Myles

.

I watched Xander from a distance. He was smiling but looked tense. I had this strange urge to hold him and make everything easy for him. Then I shook my head. I couldn't feel sorry for the enemy. Xander was the reason the last four months of my life were hell after my breakup with Simon, and now was my chance to get back at Xander, and I was going to make his life hell.

.

Xander

.

"Thank you so much for coming at the last minute. I owe you big time." I thanked the band members that Mrs. Cook had sent to help me.

"No, need to thank us, anything for Mrs. Cook. I was once a resident at her home," the band leader said as he shook my hand.

"Oh my god, you are Tristan," Ruby screamed.

"The one and only," the band leader smiled at Ruby.

"Tristan was one of the finalists in the Music Idol show," Ruby told me. She was practically glowing.

"Woo, this place is lit," one of the band members said.

"Yeah, we only got one hour before we start, so we should better get going," I said.

"I thought you said two hours on the phone?" Tristan asked. At least the other members started unloading their equipment.

"And it took you an hour to get here. Don't worry. I already have everything planned. Like, what to play and when. Glen and Eric will help you with all that," I introduced them to Tristan while I answered the emergency call from backstage.

I started running in the direction of backstage to solve some costume problem, and without looking where I was going, I slammed straight into a man's hard body.

"I'm so sorry," I started apologizing when I realized it was Myles holding me. One of his hands was around my back to support me, and the way our bodies were entangled into each other was something I didn't want to focus on. So, I stepped back immediately.

"What's the hurry? It's not like you are going to impress anyone," Myles remarked.

"I don't have time for this," I started to move, but he held my arm and made me stay in place to face him.

"Let me remind you something, Xander," he kept his big hand on my chest and paused for a second like he just noticed what he did, but he didn't remove his hand and continued, "I'm your boss, so, if I say you stay, you stay." He was so close I could feel his breath on my face, and all I could focus on was the heat of his palm on my skin through my dress shirt.

"Boss, if you see, I am in a bit of a hurry right now," I tried to step back, and he removed his hand from my chest but didn't let go of my arm.

"Is that your new band? Where did you find them?" he gestured at the band members, who were busy setting up their equipment. "Are they preparing to start a comedy show? Tell you what, my father hates comedians," okay, the band members were dressed in ripped jeans and appeared young and inexperienced, but they didn't look like comedians.

"Is that so? Well, if he hates the band, you have a fair reason to get rid of me," I smiled.

"You really think I need a reason to get rid of you?" Myles gave me that perfect smirk of his.

"Oh, I think, to convince your father to get rid of me, you'd actually have to talk to him, and something tells me you are not very keen on it," spot on. I could see in Myles' eyes how right I was.

"You think you are really that smart, Xander?" He smiled.

"Mr. Alden," I faked calling his father as I pretended he was there. Myles fell for it, and I slipped away quickly while he turned to face his father, who wasn't there. Myles watched me go, and this time I smirked at him.

I finally reached the backstage, "what is it?" I asked Sophie Alden, Myles' sister. She was sweet, nothing like Myles.

"It's mom," she said, then walked me to Mrs. Alden. This was the first time I met Mrs. Alden.

"Greetings, Mrs. Alden, I am..." I started to introduce myself, but she interrupted.

"I don't care who you are, boy. Do you really expect me to walk that ramp?" she asked.

"It wouldn't be the first time you would walk a ramp," I gave her my best smile.

"What's your name?" now she asked.

"Alexander," I replied.

"Alexander, your name sounds too big for you," of course, she was Myles' mother, "Anyhoo, Alexander, you know when was the last time I walked the ramp?"

"In 1988?" I said, and her eyes widened. "I did my research."

"Very well, then, you know I last walked the ramp over twenty years ago. How do you expect me to walk the ramp without any practice? I can fall on my face if I don't know the stage."

"You do know the stage, Mrs. Alden. It's the same show, same music, same steps," I said with confidence.

"What show?"

"I bet you would know if you see the stage." I opened the curtain and waited for her to come and see. She gradually walked to the curtain and saw the stage. I knew she recognized it immediately.

"You? It's the..." she was astonished.

"The first time you met Mr. Alden, it's the same show. You were on stage, he was the guest of honour, you were the showstopper, and that's what you are today." I could see her eyes glisten. "Do you want me to go over the steps, Mrs. Alden?"

"Alexander, I was the showstopper. I can teach you a step or two," she smiled.

"Great, let's get you into costume then."

"Costume?" I showed her the tailor-made perfect replica of the dress she had worn on that stage more than thirty years ago. I was lucky to find the show's video. One of Mrs. Alden's old friends had it in her collections.

"This is amazing; how did you do all this?" she was truly amazed and happy.

"Like I said, I did my research."

"I think you are living up to your name, Alexander," she smiled.

"Thank you, Mrs. Alden. I'll let you ladies get ready and I'll check on music."

I waited at the side of the stage as I watched Sophie Alden make a little speech I had helped her prepare. She talked about how her parents had met, and today, we will reminisce the memories of that day.

"Good job, Sophie, you are a professional. Be sure to get off the stage on your left," I communicated through the earpiece plugged into Sophie's ear. "Cue the music," I said on the other channel.

Myles came to stand next to me, and I don't know if the most disturbing thing was that Myles hated me so much that he wanted his parent's anniversary to fail or the fact that I could identify his presence by the scent of his cologne without a glance in his direction.

"I give you credit for the imagination, but you seriously think my mom would..." he stopped mid-sentence when he watched how the stage cleared when a bunch of middle-aged models in the feathered costumes walked the ramp before giving way for our showstopper, Mrs. Alden. She still had grace as she held her head high and owned the stage. I could see Mr. Edwin Alden was equally surprised and awed by Mrs. Alden as she met every beat of the music and didn't miss a step while she smiled at Mr. Alden.

The most enthralling thing was not happening on the stage but right next to me, where Myles was awestruck, watching his mom and dad with stars in their eyes. I was so proud that I made that possible.

"Lights on the floor," I said in the earpiece as the show ended. Mr. Alden walked to the stage to help Mrs. Alden off the stage, "cue the band," I said in the earpiece. The band took over the stage and started playing the 80s popular music for Mr. and Mrs. Alden as they danced to the beats on the floor, looking into each other's eyes.

"They seem happy," Myles said. It was both a surprise and longing in his voice that made him almost human, and I forgot how much I hated him.

"They loved each other when they got married," I reminded him.

"Huh, I always thought my Mom married my dad for money, so she didn't care if he cheated on her," having a mother for a drug addict, it still hurt to hear how Myles felt about his mother.

"Or maybe she loved him so much that she couldn't leave him despite the cheating," I opposed.

He laughed at that, "Or maybe you are an idealist idiot." he held my gaze, waiting, and then walked away, reminding me again why I hated him.

"Asshole," I said after him when he was gone.

The party was going well, with no actual disasters other than running out of crab cakes.

"Hey, I hear you are the new event planner. Nice work," said one of the guests, who appeared to be in his fifties.

"Thank you, Sir," I replied with a smile.

"You know, Lydia, the old planner, didn't hold a candle to your talent. Very creative you are," he squeezed my shoulder. Lydia was the previous event planner. From what I'd heard, she was good at her job.

"I appreciate the compliment, Sir," I smiled.

"You deserve it," he smiled, checking me out. "Hectic job, isn't it? You must be tired," he massaged my shoulder.

"Not much. I'm fine, really," I tried to step back, "how about I get you a drink?" I offered.

"Oh, come on, if someone deserves a drink, it's you," he grabbed my arm and walked me towards the bar, "Wow, you have strong muscles. You don't look like much, though," he winked as he felt my biceps.

"A whisky," he ordered the bartender, "what would you have, darling?"

"I am still working, so," I tried to politely step back again.

"Oh, come on, just one drink," he pushed me on the barstool, as he gripped my thigh, "there is always room for a little break," he moved his hand, feeling my thigh muscles. Okay, I wasn't stupid, I just didn't want to create a scene, everything was going perfectly until now.

"See, I'm just," I tried to push his hand away while he tried to move his hand between my legs. I wanted to break his fingers.

"Mr. Blake," Myles stepped in, and the man pulled his groping hand away.

"Hello, Myles, great party, son. Can't believe it has been that many years to your parents' marriage," the man said.

"Very hard to believe. By the way, Mrs. Blake is looking for you. I told her I saw you going to the bar with a young man," Myles smiled at Mr. Blake, and Mr. Blake got off the barstool as if he had ants in his pants.

"Oh, you didn't have to, Myles. My wife gets worried for no reason. I'll go check on her," he practically ran the other direction, and Myles took his vacant seat and accepted the whiskey from the bartender, Mr. Blake had ordered.

"So, this wasn't a total fail," he took a sip from the drink as he eyed me.

I was still irritated with what just happened, and I was nowhere ready to accept that Myles Alden had to rescue me, "I should go check on the dinner."

Before I got up, he commanded, "Sit," so I did.

"Hey, two more," he said to the bartender, and the bartender filled two glasses.

"Look, I appreciate what you did, but I didn't need rescuing. I've been raised in a group home. I know how to take care of myself," I glared at Myles.

"Didn't think you needed rescuing. I just wanted you for myself," Myles offered me one of the glasses of whiskey as he turned to face me. I gave him a quizzical look, and he added, "To talk to you, you are working for me, and so your time is mine. Have a shot," he gestured towards the drink.

"No thanks, I'm not a whisky person," I said while I pushed the glass back to Myles. "Besides, I need to go check if your parents' dinner date is going well," I tried to get up again.

"Sit down, Xander, it's over," I looked at him, confused. Was he finally firing me now?

"What do you mean?" I asked.

"I mean, nice try, but like I said, you don't know my parents as I do," I could barely focus on Myles' words over the sound of my heartbeat, which was still struggling to accept Myles wasn't my knight but an enemy when Glen's call interrupted.

"You gotta see this, buddy. It's not going well," Glen said, and I looked at Myles, who effortlessly downed the second glass of whiskey.

"On my way," I said. Myles didn't stop me this time, and I had a terrible feeling about it.

Chapter Six

I don't play to lose

.

Myles

.

I watched through the glass wall of my bedroom as the guests started to leave. Some were too drunk to move their asses from the bar, and others were making faces, gossiping as they headed to the parking lot.

Xander was trying his best to stop a few journalists from taking pictures. While making sure the drunks were getting the car rides he had arranged. He sure wasn't prepared for all the guests leaving at the same time.

I bet my Mom and Dad were either busy fighting and accusing each other of their unhappiness, or they had moved on to their respective corners of the house.

I removed my suit jacket, loosened my shirt's buttons, and made another drink when Xander barged into my room without knocking.

"See, you found my bedroom," I smiled.

Xander charged at me in full rage, "You sick asshole, you ruined your parents' anniversary so you could make me fail your stupid challenge?" he looked maddening and hot as hell as he moved closer, "what kind of a selfish asshole of a son does that to his parents?" He was in my face.

"What makes you think I did anything?" I asked.

"Don't you fucking lie to me now. Glen told me your parents were happy. They were chatting until you showed up and said something that messed up their mood."

How could someone yell at you and still look so fucking adorable?

"I said something? That's what ruined the perfect couple's happiness? Is that what you think, Xander?" I questioned.

"You did this on purpose. They were fine, they were happy, they were enjoying their date," he looked hurt, and part of me wanted to comfort him, but it wasn't my job to console my enemy, especially when he was accusing me.

"Yeah, I bet you thought after this date, they'd fall in love again and go on a second honeymoon or something," I laughed, "you are an idiot, Xander, and I am not responsible for your foolishness." I divulged.

"It's not idiotic or foolish to believe that once in love, a couple can fall for each other again. But you ruined it all because you are a selfish, self-centred, egotistic asshole who cannot think beyond himself," Xander poked his index finger to my chest as he enunciated each adjective to describe me. Something went off in my head. I held his hand and pulled him closer before he could dig a hole into my chest with that finger.

He glared at me for a few beats, but at least he shut up, "you think I'm the reason for their fight?" I asked.

"I don't think. I know it's your ego," Xander didn't step back, and I could feel his breath on my skin.

"My ego?" I asked, moving even closer, and I could see Xander took it as a challenge and didn't step down.

"You are so adamant about ruining my career that you don't see you are ruining your parents' relationship. What kind of heartless bastard spoils his parents' relationship to win a fucking challenge?" I swiftly moved my head to bring my mouth closer to Xander, and he shut up. I didn't know why I did that? Part of me desperately wanted to kiss Xander, see if his mouth tasted the same as the first time I kissed him. Or maybe it was just whisky.

I straightened myself to meet his eyes, "I didn't say anything to my parents. I just happened to be in the middle of their drama. My father had spent last night at a hotel with one of his mistresses, a so-called business associate. A reporter outed him in front of my mother, so all that shouting between my parents had nothing to do with me poisoning their special date night or that stupid challenge of yours," I could see the understanding in his eyes. Then his gaze fell to my lips before he met my eyes again, and my inside burned with a sudden awareness. I fucking wanted Xander.

"I'm sorry, I didn't know," Xander lowered his gaze, and he looked so gorgeous that I didn't trust myself with him.

"Make a note to put that on a card," I stepped away from him before I did something stupid like grab him and kiss him as if it was the last thing I could do before I died.

Xander opened the door but didn't leave, he stood there for a few seconds before he turned to face me again, "So, I won the challenge."

.

Xander

.

Myles chuckled, "Looks to me like all the guests left pretty soon," Myles gestured towards the glass wall of his room, from where I could see, other than a few drunks, hardly any guests were at the party. I knew the party ended in a disaster, and nothing could stop it from being the headline of a local business blog tomorrow, but no other event planner could prevent it from happening.

"The event was a success. It's not my fault if your father ..." I stopped myself. I had no right to say it. No matter how much I hated Myles, he didn't deserve to be mocked for his father's actions. "You can't blame me for that incident. The event was perfect," I argued.

"You are right," He continued, making another drink.

"I am?" I asked, and Myles chuckled at my response.

"Yes, Xander, This wasn't a complete failure. At least the party didn't end with my mom throwing a glass at my father or them calling each other some respectful names," Myles shrugged nonchalantly. Had it really happened, Mrs. Alden throwing a glass at Mr. Alden? I didn't have to ask to know that it did.

"I'm sorry to hear that," I could see his surprise at my response before returning to his usual smug face. Then he offered me a glass of whisky.

"Drink up, Xander. Looks like you passed the challenge."

"I did?" I stepped forward and accepted the glass from Myles.

"Looks that way," Myles said while he took a sip from his drink. And I followed his lead, but the drink was strong. It tasted like petrol. I never had anything like this before, so I coughed it out.

"Don't drink all at once," he warned and added some soda into my drink, "develop your taste," he said, and it reminded me of his time with Simon. That's exactly what he said to Simon for Sushi and that espresso ice cream, 'develop your taste.'

"I'm not Simon, Myles," I reminded him, in case he forgot, "I won't like this expensive whisky just because you like it," I held his gaze in retaliation.

"I know Xander," Myles said, and I noticed that his piercing green eyes were a shade darker in the dim light of the room. "You are not Simon. Simon had so much potential." Did he just compare me to Simon, and I didn't meet his standards?

"Potential? As in?" I was curious, not jealous, or that's what I told myself.

"Potential to be my husband, nice background, good education, wealthy family," that answer stung more than it should. It shouldn't have been a surprise. Everything was business for Myles Alden.

"Not everything is about money. Sometimes you should follow your heart," I stepped forward like he couldn't hear me from a foot away.

I noticed a slight change in his demeanour. Myles leaned towards me and lowered his voice a notch down, "Now, that's a big holiday movie scam right there. And I bet you believe in them." He moved closer to look straight into my eyes, "I can see there are big dreams of perfect love in those hazel eyes, under those thick, beautiful fake eyelashes."

"My lashes are natural. I have an Italian background," I defended. I placed the whisky glass on the minibar.

"Sure," he said as he chuckled, and I fumed. What was Myles' obsession with my lashes? Was he teasing me?

"There is nothing fake about me, Myles. You are the one who's fake," I retorted.

"What did you say?" he stepped forward, but I held my ground.

"You've heard me. Your expensive clothes may be tailor-made, but inside this suit, you are fake. I bet you can't even be real to yourself because you don't have the guts to do what you actually want. You are a calculative coward who chooses a boyfriend on the 'potential' of how well he would fit in his society. Now, that's called being fake," I charged.

"I'm warning you, Xander," he grabbed my arm and made me meet his eyes.

"Warning me of what, Myles? I'm not scared of you. Besides, you probably have to calculate risk and profit before you do anything to me," I said to his face, "I bet you never in your life did anything spontaneous. You never followed your heart. I bet you are so scared to fail that you fucking don't even know what you want."

Before I could finish uttering more insults, he pressed his mouth to mine, and everything around me stilled. When he pulled back, I could see his eyes were dark with lust as he gazed into my eyes, and I didn't even bother to consult rationality before I grabbed his fancy custom-made collar and pressed my lips to his.

And after a minute of the struggle for dominance, he started kissing me. I could tell he loved to be in control, and it didn't take him much time to hold my head and direct that kiss. I didn't only follow his lead. If he kissed me hard, I kissed him harder. If he pushed his body to mine,

I did the same. I didn't know if I was trying to make out with him or win one over him?

Man, he was fast to get rid of my suit jacket. His hands worked on my shirt. I tried to do the same, but he pushed me to his bed. I think it was the bed because all I could focus on was the hot body of Myles Alden on top of me in that unbuttoned shirt, along with the feel of his firm lips and the urgency of that fierce tongue that he pushed inside my mouth. I felt his long lashes flutter against my cheek, and my ego wanted to say, 'Ahan,' but his closeness ignited the fire inside me, blocking everything else out of my mind. He unbuttoned my pants, and I let him, but I didn't let him take my pants off completely. I pushed him so I'd be on top of him, and he let me, and then I went for his fancy belt buckle. I bet these pants cost so much. You could feel how smooth and high-quality the zipper was. And God, he was big, the domineering asshole had nothing to have a complex about. He pushed me back on the bed, so he was on top of me again.

He was such a dominating ass. I tried to get up again, but he pinned my arms on both sides, "stay still, Xander, or I'll tie you up," he ordered in his deep, dominating voice while he met my eyes. I obeyed without question. I wanted to act like I was still fighting for control, but I was so ready to give in and have him overpower me wildly when he kissed like that, and when his big hands moved down my pants, my body arched in response. He pulled my pants down all the way while I helped push my shoes off with my feet.

He wrapped his large fingers around my cock and jacked me a few times, then he ran his thumb between my slit, and I made a needy sound as my body folded forward. Myles kissed my mouth, pushing me back onto the bed. He moved one leg around me, placed his knee on the bed, and then put his other knee near my hips while pushing my leg up to position himself on top of me so our cocks and balls touched. Holding both our cocks he jacked them together, then rubbed his cock against mine. Myles wouldn't let me touch him, and I was desperate.

I moved my hips up with need, and he moved his cock against mine. I felt his delicious weight against my balls and moved with him. He pushed his tongue inside my mouth while we both chased our pleasure. When he moved his mouth down to my neck with those wet lips and took my nipple in his hot mouth, I couldn't control myself and came hard without warning. He rubbed against me faster, chasing his release and came on my stomach.

He eventually got off me and lay beside me on his huge bed. We both tried to catch our breath while staring at the ceiling to avoid looking at each other.

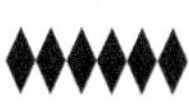

Myles

"Shit made a mistake." The magic broke with those few words out of Xander's swollen lips.

"Yeah, don't hold it back, Xander. It's not like you are going to hurt my feelings," I remarked.

I'd never seen anyone get off my bed this easily after the orgasm we shared. But Xander was Xander.

"Ha, to have feelings, you have to have a heart, Myles," Xander grabbed his pants off the floor and started dressing.

"Think you overstayed your welcome. Don't forget to shut the door behind you." Xander stopped in the middle of buttoning his shirt and glared at me.

"Gladly," with that word, he grabbed his jacket and left my room with a hard slam on my door.

"Fuck him," I whispered to myself and lay there staring at the ceiling, trying my best to write off this experience as a mistake, but I wasn't Xander. It wasn't that easy.

◆◆◆◆◆◆

Chapter Seven

One night with you doesn't make me yours

.

Xander

.

Let's not be awkward, I told myself. This was just a one-time thing with Myles, Simon's ex. *Shit.* Okay, it happened. We all make mistakes. It's done. It was just sex, wasn't even penetration. Just rubbed one against each other.

God, it was good, though. I hadn't been that excited in a long time. *Not thinking about sex,* I kept repeating in my mind, in case I ran into Myles at the office, I didn't want to picture him naked. And now I was picturing him naked. I shook my head.

Luckily for me, I didn't have to worry about running into Myles because Myles was completely ignoring me. Besides, I didn't have time to delve into this. I had work to do. I didn't want to give Myles any weapon against me.

I rechecked the blueprints and made notes. I still had to make some changes. Cathy had called the architect and booked a meeting with me to go over the designs. I didn't get enough time, but I could give him some visuals for my ideas in the *Archi* software. I went to the lobby to meet this architect when my path crossed with Myles, literally. We both froze in place when our eyes met. Then Myles examined me from top to bottom, acted as if he didn't like what he saw, and with an attitude, he went the other way. Note to self: never sleep with your Boss.

"Alexander, I thought it was you," an unfamiliar voice saved me from my thoughts going wild in Myles' direction.

"Hi, you must be Dawson Williams," that was the architect's name, I greeted him.

"The one and only," he smiled at me, "hey, Myles," he nodded to Myles, who was apparently still standing behind me.

"Dawson, what are you doing here?" Myles asked with zero courtesy.

"I came to see Xander," he answered like this visit was personal, "you never told me you are an interior designer?" Dawson gave me this big, friendly smile, and I hated to ask.

"Have we met before?" I had to ask.

"You break my heart, Xander. I guess you were too drunk that night to remember my face."

Holy shit, my mind screamed. I could feel Myles' eyes on me and the pure judgment coming my way.

I coughed, "Ah, I've got the blueprints in my office. Maybe we should discuss it over there," I didn't wait for him to follow.

"Sure, darling, anywhere you want me," Dawson followed quickly, meeting my steps. He eyed me with that full grin.

Okay, I sure had to be really drunk to do him.

We all make mistakes, don't we? Why did it sound repetitive?

I closed the door behind me as I walked Dawson to my office, "so, I created this digital work over your model, and I wanted you to see if it goes with the floor plan," I connected the projector to my laptop.

"You seriously don't remember me?" Dawson asked, watching me closely.

"No, I'm sorry," I hoped I sounded sincere. I wanted this to go smoothly.

"That's okay. You were sad, broken over some ex, and drunk. Now, I think I may have taken advantage of you. I honestly didn't mean to," Dawson laughed, but he sounded sincere.

"I appreciate you saying that. It's not a big deal," I reassured, then I mused it over, connecting dots in my head, "Oh, you are talking about the beach house party," I said, remembering that night. I didn't remember Dawson, but I remembered glimpses of that night. I wasn't exactly sad over an ex. I was sad because Myles had reminded me how pathetic I was for constantly going back to my ex after being cheated on so many times.

"Now you remember, you looked gorgeous that night. Well, you are still gorgeous," he winked, checking me out, and the door swung open on cue without a knock. Of course, it had to be Myles.

"Myles, Boss, what can I do for you?" I asked, forcing a smile.

"I want to see what you both are working on. Mind if I join?" asking, was only a courtesy because he had already taken one of the seats beside Dawson and in front of me.

"Sure, make yourself comfortable," I mumbled and operated the view for the projector.

"So, what did I miss?" Myles asked Dawson.

"Just that Xander finally remembered where we met. We were just re-imagining those moments," Dawson again winked at me with a smile, and Myles glared at me.

"Okay, so I thought I'd start with the master bedroom," I tried to get their attention to the project screen. Dawson was finally paying attention, but I could feel Myles was watching me more than what was happening on the screen. "I was thinking about installing a custom-made shelf over here. What is the size over here if we put a king-size bed in the middle?" Dawson and I rechecked the blueprints.

"We can get the wall out here, but it could delay things," Dawson said.

"No, I don't want you to change the initial plan. I think it's the same for all the houses, right?" I asked Myles. I was more of checking if he was even listening.

"Similar," he nodded, "we customize if there is a request from the client."

"Okay, so no floor changing, got it," Dawson wasn't objecting to anything, which I guess was a good thing, but Myles, being Myles, had to interfere with everything.

"I want a painting here," I showed the living room wall.

"What kind of painting?" Myles questioned.

"I don't know, haven't decided yet," I shrugged.

"How about puppies?" Dawson suggested.

"Not everyone likes puppies," Myles said to Dawson.

"Ouch, then how about kids?" Dawson said.

"Not everyone likes kids either," I said, and Myles eyed me.

"Hope you are not talking about yourself. You don't want your beauty to be wasted," Dawson flirted, which I ignored but smiled politely.

"I wasn't thinking about animals or humans for the painting. I just want something, more like Christmas theme or winter," I informed.

"That's smart," Dawson said with a grin like it was the most brilliant idea he ever heard in his life. Myles didn't say anything, but he was glaring at Dawson now, to which Dawson was oblivious.

"Okay, so moving on, I don't want much furniture in this area."

"Why not? We have so much room?" Myles interrupted.

"I thought the floor should look open and show people there is more space for them to add on stuff, plus we have a holiday theme to showcase," I explained.

"That's totally opposite of Lydia. She loved to fill every inch of the house," Dawson pointed.

Lydia was the previous designer. It wasn't the first time I had heard how Lydia used to do things.

"Maybe the house she was designing required more material," I suggested politely.

"Or maybe because she knew the market, unlike our new designer here," of course, Myles had to comment, and it wasn't the first time, I was reminded that I didn't know the market.

"Lydia did say that people buying this house were materialistic, so the more stuff, the better sell, plus the house gets sponsors," Dawson added.

"House gets sponsors anyway. It's about how we display the furniture. The better we present it, the better it sells," I argued.

"But the more stuff you have, the more you can sell," Dawson said.

"I beg to differ. Our main goal is to make the house more sellable," I countered.

Dawson went quiet, and I could feel Myles' heated gaze on me, so I quickly added, "But I'll sure make a note of it," I smiled at Dawson. "Moving on, so here is the kids' bedroom..."

I was ready to answer whatever Myles had to say, but surprisingly, he didn't say anything. "I'm leaving room for anyone who doesn't see it as a kids' room, so I'm also adding a few play features that would appeal to anyone who may want a gaming room."

"I like that," Dawson agreed. "You think outside the box. It's going to be so much fun working with you. You should come to the site with me." Dawson smiled.

"That's the plan," I grinned enthusiastically, and Myles scowled at me, which I ignored. Moving on with the slides.

"Yeah, I'm on my way," I told Simon on the phone. It was Wednesday, our Commingle night. That's what we named it when we were in college. We had decided that no matter how busy we were with our lives, we had to take one night out every month to party. Simon and my other friends were already at the bar when I got a meeting reminder on my phone.

"What the..." I checked the meeting. Apparently, Cathy had booked it with Myles about new designs at Myles' office. "Why didn't I see this before?" I had five minutes to get to the meeting.

I quickly messaged Simon, "Running late, be there in half an hour."

I took my laptop and ran to Myles' office.

I knocked at the door, "come on in," Myles said, and I did. "Shut the door behind you," he ordered, so I did.

"Something urgent, Boss?" I asked while I took the seat in front of him.

"I got your list of furniture. I don't think I can approve before I see the designs," Myles being an asshole again. The furniture was sponsored. We could change it if we had a problem.

"I already showed you the designs, and Dawson approved them," I countered.

"Dawson approved because he was more interested in getting in your pants than making this project successful," his eyes challenged me.

"Or maybe because he is an actual architect and has minored in interior design, so he knows what he's approving," I retorted.

"No, he was trying to get into your pants. Now shut up and show me your designs," he ordered, and I glared at him for a second or two. Then, I kept my laptop on Myles' desk before me.

"Can't we do this tomorrow?" I asked as I switched on the laptop. "It's already seven," I added.

"Seven? I saw you work till nine the other day," I didn't know he was in the office the other day.

"Maybe, but today I have to go." I insisted.

"What is so special about today? Do you have a date with Dawson? Or is there someone else?" he eyed me, and I couldn't help but think he was fishing.

"If you must know, it's Commingle night," I informed, and Myles stilled in reaction, sure he knew what it was. He had once or twice attended Commingle night with Simon when they had newly started dating. Myles hardly showed up after that, but Simon always did, so he had to know about Commingle night.

Myles got off his chair, walked around me, and straightened my laptop so he could see the screen, too, "show me your designs, Xander," he spoke next to my ear, and my certain body part reacted in a way I didn't want to think about, so I logged in and opened the design.

"So, the master bedroom ..." I started to say, but he interrupted, "What's that?"

"What?" I asked.

"That." he kept the finger on the screen. It wasn't a touch screen, so I double-clicked it.

"It's a photo frame," I stated.

"Why do we need a photo frame?" he questioned.

"It gives a personal touch. It's a house, and there are family pictures in the house," sure, he knew that. He was in the housing business.

"And what is that?" he touched the screen again. "that's a shelf, it's for..." I was about to explain when a message from Simon popped up on my screen with a picture, 'Where are you? We are already on the second round,' there was Simon with his new boyfriend, along with Jackie, Ben and Becca. I quickly shut the image, but obviously, Myles saw it. It was another reminder that Myles was Simon's ex-boyfriend. "So, the shelf is for easy access to remote or ..." I continued.

"That's enough, Xander," Myles said as he walked to the window and stared out the perfect downtown view of the night. "You can go. I don't want you to miss your Commingle night," he spoke without looking at me.

I shut my laptop, walked to him, and stopped a few steps behind him. I didn't know why I felt the need to say something. "I know it's new, and it's hard to understand right now, but Simon is a nice guy. I'm sure he didn't mean to hurt you," I said.

"Hurt me?" he turned to face me, "I need a heart to get hurt. Those were your words, right, Xander?" He reminded me how much of an asshole I could be at times.

"I didn't mean it like that," I retreated.

"Yes, you did. You think I don't know how many times you told Simon to dump me?" he stepped closer, and it's not that I was scared of him, but my heart sure jumped.

"Yeah, but I didn't think ..." I started to say, but he cut me off.

"What did you not think? That I'd be your Boss one day?" Myles challenged.

"Myles," I started to explain.

"Shut the fuck up, Xander. I don't need your fucking explanation," he barked.

"You know, ... this is your fucking attitude, that would never get you someone like Simon." I probably shouldn't have said that either, but I said it anyway. Okay, he was being an ass.

"Someone like Simon?" He sneered.

"Yeah, Simon is sweet, he is innocent, he is nice, and you," I paused to find words.

"And I am an asshole?" he stepped forward.

"Exactly," I stepped back only because he stepped forward, but I wasn't backing down.

"So, I don't deserve someone like Simon, so gentle, so sweet, so innocent?" he kept moving forward, forcing me to step back.

"Exactly," I wasn't folding.

"So, I deserve someone like you?" He said, and my back hit the wall, but he didn't stop moving closer, "tell me, Xander, I deserve someone like you?" he kept his hands on both sides of the wall, caging me in, "A bloody self-righteous ass, who thinks he can judge whoever he wants because he is so fucking superior to the rest of the foul-ups like me."

He talked about me in the third person, which pissed me off more. He wasn't only judging me. He was describing me.

"I'm not a self-righteous...," I started to defend, but he cut me off.

"Yeah, you are the one who can fuck his best friend's ex and pretend like nothing happened. All you have to do is write it off as a fucking mistake, and there you go, everything is perfect in your little world, and why not, since it's always other's fault. Right, Xander?" I hated him for saying that. I hated him, period.

"I didn't say it was your fault, I didn't write it off, I only said it was a mistake because you were Simon's ex and also because now I know what I can never... " I stopped myself before admitting anything and giving him the satisfaction of winning one over me. I met his piercing green eyes, and we stared at each other for a few beats before he pressed his mouth to mine. I wanted to resist, but I couldn't.

The thing with Myles is he's undeniably hot. Myles is all man, from the scratch of his stubble on my face when he kissed me hard to the hold of his tight grip on my body. Or when he pushed that hard body against mine, there was nothing in this world I could compare the feelings to. One thing for sure: Myles didn't hold back, not when he was telling me off or kissing me hard. He sure knew how to push my every button and make me painfully hard, just like now, when I kissed him back, he grabbed my hips and pulled me against his hard body.

There was no hesitation, no second thoughts. *God*, he was hot in bed or on the couch; that's where we landed. And this was the very reason people had couches in their offices. Myles kept his hand down my pants, "last chance, Xander," he breathed against my ear, "are you going to regret this in the morning?" he asked.

"Probably," I said, and the bastard squeezed me hard, making me moan. "Oh fuck," I shouted.

"You want me to stop, Xander?" Myles' long and strong fingers made it impossible for me to breathe.

"No," I whispered.

"No, what?" he bit down my neck, making me squirm.

"Don't stop," I could barely keep my eyes open when he bit down on my nipple through my shirt. Myles didn't stop. He undressed me at super speed.

And this was the best part. Myles didn't like to do anything halfway sure he took his time to give me that gradual stripping of the clothes show, when his jacket came off, when that expensive dress shirt got unbuttoned and when those tailored sexy pants came off, but in the end, he liked to get all the way naked. Getting naked with Myles was a pleasure on another level. He had this perfectly trimmed, gym-approved body with perfect muscles in the right places, and he wasn't too buffed, just right, like he was the male model in the suit magazine, just fucking hot. And fuck, Myles believed in giving maximum pleasure, like right now, his mouth could do magic. He was a fantastic kisser, and *damn*, he knew how to use that sexy mouth in more places than I could name right now.

He squeezed my balls and took my cock in his mouth. His long fingers rubbed against my hole, and my body arched in response. "I want to fuck you so fucking much right now, but I don't have supplies," he sounded desperate, and I enjoyed it.

"You can fuck my mouth," I offered, meeting his eyes without caring that I was inviting Myles Alden to overpower me.

He smiled, then moved and kissed me, pushing his tongue inside my mouth. Then he moved up and jacked his cock, while his eyes were fixed on my mouth. I bit my lip, moved forward and wrapped my mouth around his cock.

I then moved my wet lips around his cock, taking his balls in my mouth one by one. I heard him groan with need. Then I ran my tongue between his slit while I jacked some precum from his cock. He pushed me back on that couch-positioning my back to the couch's arm he moved on top of me, aiming his cock against my mouth. "Slow is good, Xander, but your little play made me a bit too desperate right now."

He ran his fingers through my hair, caressing my head, then he guided my mouth to his cock, and I took his cock in my mouth again. He started slow, but then he pushed in harder all the way to my throat.

"Umm," I made a sound, and he slowed a little.

"Okay?" he asked, running his fingers through my hair, and that gesture made my already hard cock, stand for attention.

I responded by taking him deeper into my mouth, wrapping my lips around his cock and squeezing it.

He smiled and controlled my head again for speed.

I moved my hand down to my cock and jacked myself. It felt so good giving pleasure to Myles, like I was winning this round, basking in his desperation for me.

"Can I come in your mouth?" Myles asked when he gave me room to breathe.

I nodded my approval. Myles smiled like he won the trophy, then he fucked my mouth harder and faster, controlling my head, he maintained the speed, in and out. It was damn hot when he came hard in my mouth, and I felt my release in my hands. I jacked myself some more while I watched Myles' eyes fixed on my mouth as his cum dripped through the corner of my mouth, and I tried to swallow the rest of it.

Myles was breathless. He moved around me on the couch. Moving his hand around my waist, he switched places, pulling me on top of him.

"Fuck, I wanted to do that for ages," Myles said, which surprised me, and I could feel that his body went rigid as if he realized that he said those words aloud.

Aware of the cum on my stomach, I tried to adjust my body but slipped, falling on him. "Oh," I interjected, dropping all my body's weight on him. I was pretty sure he felt the wetness of my cum.

"Shit, I didn't make you come," he regretted, and I chuckled.

"Now, you remember? I knew you were shitty in bed," I teased, and he just looked at me as if all the worries in the world consumed him.

"Kidding," I said to reassure him.

He shook his head, "Not a good joke, Xander," he said while he rubbed my head, making me rest it on his chest then he wrapped his arm around me. "Next time, I'll show you pleasure." He promised as he absently ran his hands through my hair and caressed my body like I was the most precious thing to him, and he didn't want to let go of me. I didn't want to let go of him either, so I closed my eyes and decided to live in this moment.

Chapter Eight

I won't let you break my heart

.

Xander

.

The following morning, I woke up on top of a hard body. My nose was dipped into his soft chest hair. Myles wasn't hairy, or maybe he shaved, but there were still some hairs on his chest that felt soft and nice against my skin. He also smelled good, like his expensive perfume. I looked up to see he was still asleep, and his eyelashes were thick and longer than mine, which were not fake, by the way. I remembered feeling them flutter against my skin when he kissed me hard.

Okay, gazing and admiring your one-night stand was not a good sign. With that realization, I tried to get off Myles, but he had his arm around me so tight. I thought he was worried I'd fall off the couch at night. Couldn't believe this was the same person Simon dated, or wait, maybe that's why Simon didn't want to dump Myles and didn't leave Myles for ten months because he was good in bed, which I told him he wasn't, a lie that could have hurt him. Sure, Myles knew this was not why Simon cheated on him. I felt awfully protective of Myles. Then I thought of Simon and the way he always gazed at Myles like he was his world.

"Oh fuck," the thought of Simon with Myles was enough to wake me up completely. I pushed myself off without any consideration for my partner in bed or on the couch.

"Hey," Myles complained, opening those bright green eyes.

"Sorry, I was just getting up," our eyes met, and I could see the recognition in his eyes or was that realization that we again did something we shouldn't have. "Shit, I have to go. I am meeting Dawson this morning at the site," I grabbed my briefs, my pants and started to dress. He grabbed his briefs, too, while he quickly glanced out his glass door and started dressing. I forced myself not to look.

"I can take you to the site. I am going that way," he offered. This was one of the few times Myles talked so sweetly to me, and a warning bell went off in my head.

"No, I have to go home, get a shower first," I'd never dressed so fast in my life.

"I have an apartment nearby. You can shower there," I looked at him for a second to digest what he said. Myles being nice to me was certainly not a good sign.

"No, I think I should get out of here before anyone sees us. It's still six. I got time," I started to leave, then I remembered, "Oh, I forgot," I turned, and our eyes met again, and there was something strange in Myles' eyes that I couldn't read or didn't want to read at the time. "My laptop," I said, as I grabbed it, "see you around," I ran out the door without another glance toward Myles. I scanned my card and let myself out the main entrance towards the parking lot.

I placed my laptop in the car, rested my back on its door, closed my eyes and inhaled the fresh air.

"Don't do that," I said to myself. "He was courteous, but he doesn't care for you, don't fucking fall for Myles Alden. No, not in this lifetime, never," I told myself, jumped in the car and drove back to where I belonged, the lower side of the town.

After showering and driving at full speed, I finally reached the site and met Dawson outside the model home. "I'm so sorry, Dawson, I just got caught up with something and..."

"Hey, no sweat, it's not like I'm going anywhere. I'm rooted in place," I didn't understand that for a second, "I mean the house, it's planted in place," he laughed, and I felt relaxed.

"Thanks, man, the house looks almost complete," it looked beautiful. Dawson was very talented.

"You are right, 'almost.' We still have a few things to tweak but should be fine for the open house date. It's in January, right?" he asked.

"You are kidding," I gave him a quizzical look. There was no way he didn't know the deadline.

He laughed again, "Yeah, I know it's December 20th. I'm just pulling your leg," he touched my shoulder.

"When do you think you'll begin painting? I'll send you the final list of paints. I need to see the sample of paints not just on the computer, you know, but on the surface," I informed.

"There's still time for paint. But you seem impatient," he commented while tapping my chest.

"I just want to get the house set up so I can work on the Christmas theme, the open house event," I reminded him.

"Hey, no worries, being impatient is not a bad quality," he winked, and I tried my best to respond with a polite smile.

"So, can we go inside?" I asked.

"There is still some work going on. I can show you a couple of rooms. But if you come Thursday morning, I'll be able to show you a whole lot more," again with a wink.

"So, the day after tomorrow?" I confirmed as I noted in my calendar on my phone.

"Yeah, but early morning would be best," he said.

"Okay," I nodded.

"I can show you the backside right now," Dawson offered.

"That'll be great," I smiled.

The house was big, and the surrounding area was large, with a more oversized backyard, perfect for the Christmas event. Very few builders offered an actual house as a model home, like this one. It was at the actual site. Similar homes were being built on this site. If everything went well during this opening event, all those houses should be sold before completion. I started to make some notes on my existing designs on the laptop.

"So, you are seeing anyone?" Dawson asked. I can't say I didn't see this question coming. "I mean, if you are not doing anything this Saturday, I would like to take you out for dinner."

It would have been much easier to lie, "Not sure right now. Sometimes new event requests come last minute," I said casually.

"But I thought you were full-time working with Eldwine," he asked.

"I'm just a contractor," I shrugged.

"Wow, and they gave you the corner office?" I smelled a bit of jealousy in Dawson's words, but I acted as if I didn't acknowledge it.

"It's just temporary," I said politely.

"For this project, of course, but you are very talented. I'm sure they would keep you around," he smiled.

I shrugged again. I wasn't sure what to say or where I stood with Eldwine Industries.

"So, if you are unsure about Saturday, we can meet any other night, go for drinks or dinner?" Dawson was sure persistent.

"I'm not sure right now, but I'll let you know," I smiled, and he gave me a stern look.

"Of course, you have my cell number. Let me know. I'll go check on the construction."

Dawson did not look happy, and the last thing I wanted was to have a conflict with the head architect.

It was a long drive back to the office, but I had to enter the changes into *ArchiSoft*, and since Myles forbade me to take the precious blueprints outside, I had to do it in the office.

When I reached the office, everyone was going home for the day. "Xander, come to my office," Myles came out of his office to order me to come inside using his index finger, which just fumed me. I wasn't a fucking cocktail waitress. I was exhausted and was going to give him a piece of my mind.

When I entered his office, he shut the door behind me and rolled the blinds on the glass door, then he leaned against the very door and examined me with those piercing eyes from head to toe, and my body started to react. My heart started to beat a bit faster. Two could play this game. I walked backward on my feet and similarly examined Myles. Myles was dressed in his expensive grey trousers and looked impeccable in that black dress shirt, posing like a perfect model on a magazine cover.

"What took you so long?" he inquired, breaking the silence.

"I was at the site. What do you think?" The site was a two-hour drive from the office, and this was rush hour.

He again assessed me from top to bottom, "thought you stopped for a quickie with Dawson. Did you, Xander?" he scowled at me with a challenge in his eyes.

The question infuriated me. How could I ever forget this was Myles Alden?

"Of course, a dickhead like you cannot possibly think beyond ..." I started to say when he moved towards me, kept his finger on my mouth and shushed me. Okay, that should have angered me more, but it fucking aroused me. The way his fingers grazed my lips and the focus of his eyes on me, he looked like a definition of sensuous.

"I know this is becoming kind of our foreplay, but can we once fuck without fighting?" He met my eyes with a question.

"What?"

Okay, sure, we had sex, but we didn't exactly plan it or talk about it.

"Yeah, I'd been thinking of you and that couch all day," he moved his finger down to my neck. If you like, we can get more comfortable. We can go to my apartment." This was the second time he mentioned his apartment in one day, "I've got a shower there. You look like you can use one," Myles continued in that deep, sexy voice, and sure, moving his finger down my shirt wasn't making it easy for me to call to my dignity if I had any. That was another question.

"Shower sounds good," that's all I could say at that moment. I didn't know how to talk to Myles without screaming my lungs out or being furious.

"Good, let me get my jacket." He said, and the smile he gave me was precious. I didn't know he could ever smile like that. He was so fucking hot, and I was so damned.

Myles

Xander didn't look very comfortable on our way to my car and during the ride to my apartment. He kept checking if anyone was watching us, which had started to piss me off a little.

"We should do a takeout. What do you like to have?" I asked.

"Or we can order a pizza," he suggested.

"I thought you didn't like pizza," that just slipped out of my mouth. Rule number one, don't tell a guy, you noticed him too much. But with Xander, all my rules were already out the window.

"How do you know?" I could feel his eyes examining me in the darkness of the car.

"I have a good memory, Xander, unlike yourself," I replied, deflecting his scrutiny.

"I have a good memory," he countered, as always, and I could no longer say I hated it.

"Oh, so, you only have a bad memory when it comes to who you bed with?" I teased. From what I gathered, Xander clearly didn't remember Dawson and obviously didn't know we had met before.

I watched him slightly move away from me towards the window, "I thought you said you live close by," he complained, looking out the window.

"I do. Just making a D tour," I made a turn into a Chinese takeout place. "You like Chinese, right?" Even though I asked, I knew what Xander liked, which was a disturbing realization that I had watched Xander more closely than Simon during all those friends' get-togethers.

Xander reluctantly followed me to the restaurant, then glanced around to see who was there or if anyone was watching us.

"Who are you worried about?" I finally asked after placing our order.

"What?" he asked.

"Let me rephrase it. Who do you not want to know about us?" I questioned.

"There is no us, Myles," he sneered. Okay. That didn't sit right with me, but I ignored my feelings.

"Fine," I lowered my voice and spoke close to his ear, "who do you not want to know we are fucking," then I met Xander's eyes, which looked a bit more golden than hazel in this light.

"Simon," he stated like it was apparent. Again, he looked around. Simon lived in the same area as I did. Anyone could see us together and tell Simon.

"I'm not dating Simon anymore," I said. I was free to be with whomever I wanted.

"Simon's my best friend, and you are his ex," he finally looked me in the eyes. "Do you ever think beyond yourself, Myles?" he remarked, and our eyes got locked into each other.

If he was so worried, why was he with me? The thought occurred, but I didn't voice it. I didn't want Xander to feel more guilty and leave. I wanted him, needed him.

The girl at the counter announced my name, interrupting us.

I watched Xander dig into his dinner. He was not a fan of chopsticks. Xander tasted every single dish, from spicy garlic chicken to sweet nuggets, which I didn't even know why I ordered. He was starving. I doubted he had anything for lunch or breakfast since he ran pretty fast from my office this morning. Watching Xander eat was such a treat. I couldn't take my eyes off him. He looked so yummy in my sweats and smelled so delicious with the mixed scent of my shampoo and body gel. I don't think if those products ever smelled this good on me, or, I would have been compelled to buy their shares.

"So," he tried to say something with his mouth full while he rolled the sleeves of my shirt that he was wearing, and it kept getting in the way of his fork. I held his wrist and felt his soft skin on the pads of my fingers, then I moved to properly roll his sleeves, one hand at a time. Xander watched me quietly, and once I was done, I met his surprised golden eyes. His lips looked so red and delicious with that red sauce from the chicken, and I was dying to taste him.

"So," Xander repeated, "you usually feed your hookups?" Okay, Xander, being Xander, had to bring me down to reality. It didn't matter how homely Xander looked on my couch in my sweats. He was not mine.

"You looked hungry and tired. Thought I'd feed you first," I shrugged.

"Very thoughtful, so what do you want to do now, watch a movie, cuddle until we fall asleep in each other's arms?" He mocked and batted his eyes.

"That's not a bad idea," I smiled and moved to sit beside him, facing the T.V. I picked the remote to turn on the T.V., "What's your favourite genre," I scrolled through the movie list.

"You are joking," he said with shock and stared at me, but I kept my eyes on the screen.

"No, I haven't seen a movie in a long time. I think we should give it a try, and while we are at it, we should cuddle right," I pulled him closer. His slender body fit in with mine, and he felt damn good in my arm "So, tell me, which movie do you like?" I asked, and he rested his head on my shoulder.

"I don't know. I'm already tired. I usually fall asleep searching for the movie." He said, cozying up to me like a cat, and I chuckled.

"Horror?" I asked.

"No!" he glared at me, and I couldn't help but laugh at his expression.

"Okay then, horror it is. What do you think about '*Behind the door*', '*How many left?*' oh, how about the classic '*Chucky, the doll*'?"

"I'm warning you," Xander scowled at me, and I laughed.

"I think '*Behind the door*' is the best option," I clicked play.

"No! I'm going to kill you," Xander closed his eyes, kept his forehead on my shoulder and held me tight. And then there was this first sound effect in the movie.

"Please, shut it off," Xander begged, and I stopped the movie when I noticed he was shaking, so I held him close and hugged him.

"I'm sorry, I didn't mean to scare you so much," the movie hadn't even started. I'd never seen anyone so scared of a horror movie. I rubbed his back and tried to calm him.

"Group home kids prank gone wrong," those few words said it all. I could feel the dampness of his tears on my skin. I didn't want to push for more information. I only wanted to comfort him.

"I'm sorry, Xander," I said again and ran my hand through his hair. I kissed him on the side of his face, sweaty forehead, and damp cheeks, and then I kissed his lips. I didn't want to dominate him today. I wanted him to feel safe.

"The bigger kids locked me in the theatre with Sleepy Hollow. I was eight. Those loud sounds still haunt me." He whispered.

"It's okay. You are safe now," I reminded Xander that he wasn't in danger. His body started to calm down.

I kissed him softly and let him decide what he wanted. He slightly opened his mouth to let me in. I held his face and pushed my tongue inside his mouth to get that sweet taste of his. Xander wasn't like anyone I'd ever been with. There was so much hunger. I wanted him so badly. Every time I thought, this is it, once I have Xander, I won't crave him anymore, but no, I couldn't have enough of him. He wasn't a fucking chocolate. Xander was a drug, and I was addicted. I grabbed his hand and walked him to my bed. And I swear he looked so good in my bed, like he truly belonged there. I took off his shirt and kissed his chest, then dragged my lips down to his navel, sucking his navel, and his body arched in response like a perfect reward. I didn't know pleasing your partner could feel so good. Xander was so sexy and challenging. Pleasing Xander was equally rewarding as reaching my own orgasm.

I pulled his sweats down and took his cock in my mouth. Then I kissed his shaft down to his balls. Pushing his legs up, I ran my tongue between his ass cheeks.

He whimpered with need.

Jacking his cock, I pushed my finger inside his hole, and he moaned. I moved my mouth down to the hole, kissing it. I ran my tongue inside his tight restraints, making him lose his mind.

"Oh fuck, Myles," I loved my name on his desperate lips.

I took his balls in my mouth and sucked. Then I kissed his crown and ran my tongue between his slit. His hips buckled in response. I took him all in my mouth and sucked harder.

"Myles, have to..." He breathed out.

I knew what he needed. "It's okay, fuck my mouth," I told him.

He looked at me with surprise through those hooded eyes. I pushed my finger inside his hole, and he moaned again. And I took his cock in my mouth and let him set the pace. He moved faster with desperation like his life depended on it, and when I squeezed his balls. He came hard in my mouth, and I swallowed every drop.

He was out of breath and sweaty. I lay beside him and pulled him closer. He looked at me with awe. Then he looked at my hard cock.

"I'll suck you," he tried to rise, but I pushed him down on the bed.

"No," I said, and his eyes widened. Then I didn't suggest what I wanted to. Tonight was about Xander's pleasure. "Just need your hand," I smiled, laying beside him. I grabbed his hand and directed it to my cock. He was momentarily astonished, then turned towards me and started jacking me while he moved up to kiss me. With Xander's hands on me and those soft lips on mine, it didn't take long for my release to come. I hugged him while I waited for my heart to calm. I ran my fingers through his soft hair and closed my eyes.

Xander

I woke up in the softest linen the man ever made. The bed smelled so delightful, like Acquadi Giorgio Armani. My eyes flung open at the realization I was in Myles Alden's bed yet again. Well, at least it was a bed this time.

Okay, this was becoming a bad habit. It was one thing to have sex with an enemy. It was another to sleep in his bed. I shifted to sit up to see Myles sleeping next to me. He looked so hot and sexy. In this daylight, it was hard to believe Myles Alden sucked me and swallowed my cum and the way he held me after, it was like a dream. Looking at Myles' slightly parted mouth, I was tempted to wake him up with kisses, but I stopped myself because that would be crossing a line. I shouldn't have stayed overnight. I moved away from the temptation to look for my clothes and my pride.

"Shit," I exclaimed, my clothes were in no condition to be worn again. I had been at the construction site all day yesterday. "I've got to start carrying extra clothes," I made a mental note.

"That's a wise idea," Myles said.

I was startled at his voice and turned to look at him, and damn, no one should have a right to look this good in bed hair.

"Yeah, only if I thought of it earlier. Now, I have to drive all the way home and then drive back here," I huffed at the thought of driving.

"You can borrow my clothes," Myles said.

"Excuse me?" I thought I didn't hear him right.

"Yeah, the sweats looked good on you, and I have plenty of clothes," he couldn't be serious. I looked at him for a second for a hint of a joke when he added, "All my work clothes are in this closet," he pointed at the closet.

"Oh sure, because nothing screams like I'm shagging my boss than showing up to work in his oversized, ten thousand dollar Armani suit." I mocked.

"Some of my suits are Brioni," he replied, and I just stared at him with an open mouth, "Okay, I also have casuals."

"No thanks, I wouldn't want to break the precious dress code at the office," I started dressing in what I had.

"Boy, are you always this cheery in the morning?" he commented.

"I guess it depends on the company," I retorted, and then we just stared at each other. I know there was no need for a comeback, but with Myles, I could never control my tongue or apparently any parts of my body. With that frightening realization, I quickly added, "I should go." I turned away, fighting against whatever magic was pulling me towards Myles.

I slipped my feet in the shoes when he interrupted, "Wait, I thought we could go get some breakfast. There is a café downstairs. I'll get ready in a few," Myles got out of bed, and I did my best not to stare at his naked body.

"No," I forced myself to look at his face when he stopped to listen, "I mean, we can't. Simon lives a few blocks from here. Anyone can see us and tell Simon," I objected, and he scowled at me for a few uncomfortable seconds. I couldn't tell if his sudden anger was for me or Simon. Then he nodded, grabbed his briefs and covered himself, looking anywhere but at me.

"Don't forget to lock the door behind you on your way out."

So, the anger was for me. I knew I pissed him off, especially since he shut the bathroom door behind him with more bang than needed. I didn't want to read too much into it, or I'd start seeing things that were not there. Myles accused me of being an idealist. I was anything but an idealist. I knew this arrangement between Myles and me was just that, 'an arrangement.' We satisfied each other's sexual needs, nothing more, nothing less. So, I gathered the rest of my things and quietly left his apartment.

Chapter Nine

.

I will never fall for you...

.

Myles

.

I was more pissed than I should have been. What did Xander call it? 'A hookup,' that's precisely what it was, "a hookup." I told myself, but I was angry more than I was convinced. "No, Xander is not right for me," I reminded myself. Xander didn't fit the profile of my perfect boyfriend. My father would never be happy. I laughed at myself. Xander was right. Did I ever do anything in my life because I wanted it? "Only with Xander," then and now. The first time I met Xander, I broke all the rules and let a street kid sweep me off my feet. And now, again, it's Xander. But then Xander was the reason why I swore to myself not to step outside those boundaries of social class. Those differences were there for a reason.

Cathy knocked at my door, interrupting my thoughts. "Yes, Cathy," I invited her in.

"I've been trying to call you. Your phone is still on voice mail," she pointed at the phone on my desk.

"Oh, I forgot to change it," I clicked on my office phone. "Anything urgent?"

"Your boyfriend, Simon, is here to see you," I was so shocked I didn't correct Cathy, "Should I let him in?"

"Ah, yeah, sure, let him in," I absently allowed.

She smiled and left.

"Myles," Simon walked all the way to me, and I greeted him with a quick hug since I didn't know how you greeted an ex who had cheated on you and then proudly dumped you in front of all his friends.

"Simon, I'm sure surprised to see you," I offered him to sit.

"I'm surprised, myself," he said, and I waited for him to sit. "I'm sorry," he apologized.

"Simon," I started to say...

"Let me say it, or I won't be able to." Simon interrupted, so I nodded and let him continue, "I have no excuse for how I treated you. I cheated on you, and then I was so proud of it. There is nothing to be proud of cheating. I was wrong, and I understand that now," Simon looked sincere. He was never good at lying anyway.

"Simon, it's okay. It's not entirely your fault. Maybe I didn't treat you right," I was stunned at my own words. A few days ago, if I had seen Simon, I would have insulted him. Hell, I wouldn't even have let him in my office, let alone tell him it wasn't entirely his fault.

"Myles, you are so sweet. I'm glad you understand." Simon smiled with relief. "I also wanted to tell you I am here because I took your advice," he added.

"What advice?" I asked.

"You were right. I'm not a good family lawyer. I should have stuck to the family business, so I am now studying property law," Simon smiled, and I felt guilty.

"Simon, I shouldn't have tried to boss you. You are smart. You can make your own decisions."

"I know, I can. My decision is influenced, but I've never felt more sure. Property law is for me, and my father is guiding me," Simon reassured.

"That's good. I am happy for you," I smiled.

"Wait, there is more," He said.

"I am listening."

"Your dad offered me to come and assist your property lawyer, Mr. Chin," Simon informed, and I froze for a second, thinking of Xander and how worried he was about Simon finding out about us.

"Okay," I nodded anyway, knowing where this was going.

"Before I accepted this job, I wanted to see if you were okay with it?" Simon searched my face with hope, and I had this opportunity to refuse, but that would be an asshole thing to do, which wouldn't go well with Xander. Seeing it was Xander, I was trying to please. I had to do the right thing by his best friend, or he'd be more pissed at me.

"Simon, I am more than okay. In fact, I'm happy for you," I smiled.

"You are?" he was surprised.

"Hundred percent," I assured him.

"So, you wouldn't mind joining me for dinner to celebrate our new work relationship and maybe a new friendship," he gave me his sweet smile, and I gave in. Simon was sweet. Whatever happened, it wasn't entirely his fault. I knew I wasn't the best boyfriend.

"Absolutely, let's go right now, my treat, in honour of your new job," I grabbed my jacket.

"Wow, seriously?" He cheered up.

"Never been more serious," I smiled.

"You seem different," he commented.

"Different good?" I opened the door for Simon.

"Definitely different good," he smiled.

"Ouch, so I was that bad before?" I asked.

"Where do you want me to start," Simon said, and I laughed.

Xander

It took me a couple of hours to return to the office from driving back and forth. I noticed Myles' office door was locked. I could tell he was in a meeting with someone, but I couldn't see who it was. I went to my office and started updating my designs with the notes from yesterday. It was five when I was done touching up the design plans. I forgot about lunch again. I thought of Myles and the time we had yesterday. It almost felt like a date. Would it be going too far if I asked him for dinner? Not as a date, of course, just to eat together, like yesterday, maybe. God, I was overthinking it. It was just food, we all needed to eat. I walked out of my office and noticed that Myles' office was locked, and there was no one inside.

"Looking for Myles?" Cathy asked.

"Ah, yeah, I thought I'd show him the designs. Is he gone already?" I asked.

"Yeah, his boyfriend came to see him, and they left together," The shock I felt had to be at least a thousand watts because I couldn't hear what Cathy said afterward. "They look so good together," Cathy was saying when I re-tuned.

"What?" I asked like an idiot.

"I said, if it's urgent, you can always message Myles. He is really good with text, unlike Mr. Edwin Alden, his father. I assisted him once when his assistant was on vacation. I sure never want to repeat that experience." Cathy chatted.

"Yeah, yeah," I barely heard what Cathy was saying, "thanks, Cathy, nothing urgent. It can wait."

"Okay, then, I'm leaving for the day. See you later," she smiled, grabbing her bag.

"Yeah," I tried to smile and answered her 'good night' as I watched her leave.

Myles Alden had a boyfriend. But it had only been five months since Simon and I assumed he was single. It should have never shocked me, but like the idiot I was, I let myself be fooled by a man like Myles. What angered me the most was that I'd been thinking all day that I may have hurt Myles when I rejected his offer for breakfast. Oh yeah, as if a little bug like me could ever affect Myles Alden. He was fucking cheating on his boyfriend with me.

What the hell did he think I was? Some cocktail waitress he picked off the floor. He didn't owe any explanation to? I was going to make him pay.

Myles

"I overreacted. I wasn't in my senses, and I am so sorry," Simon apologized for the third time, and he only had a few drinks so far.

"It's okay. I probably deserved it," I repeated Xander's words only to dampen Simon's guilt.

"No, you didn't. I guess you have been nice to me in your own way. You just don't know how to romance a guy. I had no right to punish you for it," What Simon said got me thinking. I knew I'd been a terrible boyfriend to Simon, but my thoughts involuntarily went to Xander and how I wanted to do everything right for him, which was absurd because Xander wasn't my boyfriend.

"You didn't punish me. All you did was break up with me, and breakups are never pleasant," I tried to lessen Simon's guilt.

"You are so understanding, Myles. I shouldn't have ended things the way I did. Inviting all my friends and insulting you was very wrong of me. Even Xander said, ..." he paused and shook his head.

"What did Xander say?" I asked.

"Xander? Oh, he was ... is he working with you?" Simon asked.

"Yeah, he is. So, what did Xander say?" I moved forward to ask again. Simon looked buzzed.

"Wow, we'll be all working together. That's so cool," he said, taking another sip from his drink.

"Yes, we will," I thought about it for a second. "Xander would be thrilled," would we have to sneak out to have sex.

"You are a prick," Simon said, and for a second, I thought he heard my thoughts.

"Excuse me?" I asked.

"That's what Xander said," Simon clarified.

"Of course," I muttered, picking up my drink again.

"But you didn't deserve to be cheated on," Simon added.

"What?"

"Xander said I was wrong, and nothing could ever justify me cheating on you," he said guiltily.

"He said that?" I asked, trying to hold my smile.

Simon nodded more times than needed.

"I was wrong, I'm sorry," he said again.

"It's okay, Simon, you've already said it," I smiled.

"You are so understanding, Myles." He smiled.

"I've always been understanding, Simon," I smirked.

"No, Myles, you weren't. Part of the reason why we broke up," he said.

"You mean part of the reason why you dumped me," I corrected.

"I am trying to be polite," he sniggered.

I laughed in response. Even I couldn't believe I was being so understanding and reasonable right now. A few days ago, I would have used this opportunity to insult Simon, but I just didn't care today.

"You seem different," he said again.

"Different good," Simon had already repeated several times, so I prompted.

"Yeah, you are listening to me," he said with awe.

"God, I was a jerk, wasn't I?" I realized.

"That's putting it mildly," Simon said, and I laughed.

My phone pinged in my pocket at the time.

"Excuse me," I checked my phone and read the two words, "Fuck U," a text from Xander.

"Everything okay?" Simon asked, and I realized I was frowning at my phone.

"You want to order another drink? I'll just be back." I didn't wait for Simon to respond and made my way out the door as I rang Xander.

"Got your text," I said as soon as Xander received my call.

"You are calling to tell me your phone service is working?" his words slurred, and I couldn't help but smile.

"No, just calling to tell you I'm a top," I whispered into the phone.

"You think this is funny, asshole?" Okay, he was in one of those moods when he was pissed at me. It used to irritate me, but lately, everything about Xander brought this goofy smile to my face and turned me the hell on.

"Okay, what did I do this time?" I asked.

"Fuck you," he repeated.

"Xander," he disconnected. Okay, he was really pissed.

"Don't hang up on me," I ordered as soon as Xander answered the call again.

"Is that an order, Boss? What else can I do for you? Lick your boots?" Xander retorted.

I chuckled, which I knew pissed Xander even more. "Why boots? Don't you think there are better things to lick?" I teased.

"Don't fuck with me, Myles," now I knew I seriously screwed up something.

"Xander, if you won't tell me what I did ... hello?" he hung up on me again, "Oh come on," now he wasn't answering my call.

"Is everything okay?" Simon surprised me. I had forgotten about Simon. How could I forget about Simon? Xander was right. I was an asshole.

"Yeah, my ..." I stared at my phone. I almost blurted Xander's name. "I just came out to make a phone call," I said.

"I see that. To be honest, I feared you abandoned me," Simon looked soberer now.

"Simon, I would never do that to you," I reassured him, even though I had just forgotten about him.

"I'm getting that. But I didn't know you were dating again," Simon searched my eyes.

"Dating? No, not dating," why did it sound like a nervous lie?

"No need to lie to me, Myles. I'm a big boy. I can handle it. Besides, I'm the one who ended things. But it looks like you just had your first fight," Simon commented.

"First fight? It's more like we fight less now. He is this ball of rage, always ready to blow up in my face. I don't understand half the things that make him angry. I'm just always thinking, okay, what the fuck did I say now? And when I ask him, I never get a straight answer just like right now. I asked him, what the fuck did I do if he'd just tell me I could probably fix it. But, no, I'm sure he's just sitting somewhere pouting. Though every time he's angry, he looks so tempting that I can't help... " I coughed, realizing what the fuck I was going on about and who the fuck I was talking to.

"Okay, I'm officially jealous," Simon said, but he smiled.

"Sorry, Simon, I didn't mean to say all that to you," I apologized.

"No, I get it. I kept hoping that you would once talk about me like that during our relationship, but you never did. *He* must be special." His eyes examined me.

"It's nothing like that. It's nothing serious, Simon," I thought I was telling the truth, but my heart didn't seem to believe it.

"If that's not serious for you, then what is, Myles? I hate to admit, but you sounded like you are in love."

Simon pointed. Okay, that wasn't true. I was ready to deny it, but the words got stuck in my mouth, and I just stared at Simon.

"I hate you." Xander's text grabbed my attention once again.

"So, who is he? Have I met him? I so fucking hope I haven't. It'd be weird, like as if you were waiting for me to get out of your way." Simon sighed, and I just stared at him. Then he laughed, "Sorry, I know I don't have any right to make such demands when I am the one who broke up with you for someone else," Simon looked at me with pleading eyes.

"Everything is alright with your relationship? I hope he is treating you better than I was," I asked. I genuinely felt sorry for being an ass to Simon.

"Yeah, everything's great. You should probably get that," he pointed at my phone.

"Yeah, he's in a mood. Mind if I cut this meeting short?"

"Yeah, no worries, I'll be seeing you at work anyway," he started to walk away.

"Do you need a ride?" I asked as an afterthought.

"No, I'll call a cab."

"You sure? I'm not being a prick with you again, am I?"

"You don't owe me anything anymore, Myles. See you at the office, boss," he waved me goodbye. After that nasty breakup, I never thought I'd ever be able to get over Simon, but right now, all I could focus on was Xander and why the fuck he was so pissed?

Chapter Ten

I'll let you play me a little longer

·

Xander

·

I sat on the steps of my home with a half-finished bottle of vodka in my hand. The bottle was a gift from Uncle Luca, one of the other renters I shared the apartment with. He'd made this very vodka at home with potatoes and wanted me to sell it for him at one of my events. I told Uncle Luca I couldn't do that without a license, but he kept bribing me with these bottles that I never drink, but today was an exception. Uncle Luca's vodka wasn't bad, but it smelled weird. I took another sip when my phone rang. When it rang for the fifth or sixth time, I picked up to look at the caller. Myles' name flashed on the screen, and I stared at it until it disappeared.

'I hate you,' I had texted him, and I meant it. He used me. Did he think I was some cheap rent boy he could use whenever he wanted? There were text messages from Myles that I didn't bother to read and concentrated on my drink. I looked around my neighbourhood only to realize the difference between Simon and me. Simon had a lovely, lavish apartment at the high end of the town. All our get-togethers were always at Simon's place because it was big, beautiful and safe. I watched a few guys beating the crap out of another guy at the side alley of my house. I quickly looked away when one of them yelled, "What are you looking at?"

Then I saw a bunch of guys across the street, trying some new street drug called '*Oxyhigh*.' How did I know that? I was offered to try one, just like this vodka. I couldn't say I had never tried drugs before. Hell,

I sold it, but that was a long time ago. I didn't stop drugs by choice. I stopped because I almost died. I used to have these memory lapses, but I didn't care until the doctor warned me that the drugs were in my blood. I was born with it. My mother was a drug addict, and who knew what my father was? Even though my mother had promised she was sober for the nine months she had me, the blood results said otherwise. The doctor warned me that I would kill myself if I continued this lifestyle. There wasn't much I could do about the past, so I focused on my future. Since that day, I'd never touched any drugs.

"Hey," I didn't have to look up to see it was Ryan. I even recognized his old sneakers as he touched my boot with his old runners. "I thought it was you. Look at those fancy clothes. I barely recognized you," I looked up to meet his eyes.

"I barely recognize myself," I slurred.

He sat next to me, "you are alright?"

"Yeah, I'm just perfect," I took another sip from the bottle.

"You look down. Did someone hurt you?" always so concerned was Ryan.

"I forgot for a moment who I was, and someone showed me my ugly reflection in the mirror," I rested my back to the door.

"What? That's not true, Xander. You are anything but ugly. You are one of the prettiest guys I've ever seen and trust me, I've seen plenty."

"I'm sure," I frowned.

"Hey, don't be like that. I don't cheat anymore. I never meant to, you know, and I am sorry. I'm just not the relationship type, you know, that's all," Ryan placed his hand on my leg.

"Hmm," I smiled. Ryan may be a cheating bastard, but he never made me feel like a cheap whore like Myles did.

"So, who hurt you?" he asked.

I shook my head. I didn't trust myself not to cry.

"Some rich asshole, I bet," he said knowingly.

Tears involuntarily formed in my eyes. I blamed it on the vodka.

"Give me his name and address, and I will show him what it's like to hurt my friend," Ryan said protectively.

I laughed at that.

"Want me to give you a blowjob?" Ryan offered.

I shook my head again.

"Oh, come on, it'll help you relax," he insisted while he massaged my shoulder.

"Leave it, Ryan," I moved away from him, resting my back on the side of the door. I focused on the moving club lights in the sky when a car screeched on the road, disturbing my two minutes of peace. For a second, I couldn't believe what my eyes were seeing. When I focused on the car, I realized it was Myles in his fancy BMW.

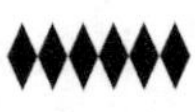

Myles

The GPS indicated I arrived at my destination. I hit the break when I saw Xander sitting at the steps of one of the old houses with some large-sized tattooed man. I saw red when my eyes focused on that man's hand placed on Xander's leg.

I got out of my car and made it at full speed towards Xander.

"Xander," I said a little louder than I intended to.

"Myles, what're you doing here?" I saw a half-empty bottle in his hand, and the tattooed man sitting next to him still hadn't removed his hand. The man looked like a bloody convict. I glared at him when he smiled and moved his hand slightly upwards on Xander's leg. Which Xander didn't seem to notice.

"What the fuck are you drinking? It smells like shit." I said.

"Fuck off, Myles, you don't tell me what to do," Xander retorted.

"I'm your boss, I do tell you what to do. Now get up, and let's go with me," I ordered.

"It's Friday," he said, "or Saturday?" he looked confused.

"It's still Friday, sweetie," the tattooed man said, and I couldn't explain the anger I felt.

"Right. I'm home. Why would I go with you, Boss?" Xander questioned.

"He's your boss?" the tattooed man interrupted again.

"He's an ass," Xander replied, and the tattooed man laughed as if it was hilarious.

"You are drunk, Xander. I don't want you to wake up tomorrow and not remember what you did or who you did," I glared at the tattoed man.

"Woo, is that comment directed at me, bro?" the man said.

"Don't fucking bro me, convict," I uttered, and the tattooed man stood on his feet.

"What did you say?" the man charged at me.

"Hey, stop," Xander tried to step between us and almost lost balance, and we both grabbed him.

"Take your fucking hands off him," I pulled Xander towards me and warned the tattooed man.

"You are out of your mind, suit. You know who you're talking to?" at least he let go of Xander.

"I'm not fucking scared of you, convict," I challenged. I was clearly not in my senses.

"You fucking should be, you may be a rich asshole, but this is my area," the fucking convict threatened me.

"Ryan, back off, and shut up, Myles," Xander ordered while his back touched me, calming me a little. "Come on," Xander grabbed my hand and walked me to my car.

We drove a few miles in silence, "are you still awake," I asked Xander while I kept my eyes on the road.

Xander made a sound like I disturbed his sleep and then steered towards me, putting his back to the car door and folding one of his legs on the seat. He looked at me straight. I was amazed at how he did it with the seat belt still on.

"Did that all just happen?" he asked.

"It did happen, and can you sit properly? It's not safe. We are on the freeway."

Of course, he ignored my instructions.

"What did you call Ryan?" he scrutinized me.

"Convict," I stated as it was since he looked like one.

"Shit Myles, rule number one, you don't talk like that to a guy like Ryan, in his area," Xander asserted.

"You think he'll be a problem for you?" I worried. I didn't like what I saw. The neighbourhood didn't look safe for Xander.

"Me? No, Ryan is harmless to me, but you, he could seriously damage your pretty face," he said.

"Pretty?" I laughed, "I'd prefer handsome," I met his eyes for a second. "I think you underestimate me. Maybe I would have damaged his ugly face," okay, the guy wasn't ugly. He was good-looking, and that was part of the problem.

"Seriously, Myles, it's better to keep your ego in your pants when it comes to guys like Ryan."

"You think I couldn't take him?" Okay, maybe that was pure ego. "I'm a black belt, you know, and I was a quarterback in college."

Xander laughed. "I bet. Parents' money is well spent," he mocked. I couldn't deny it. Xander, being Xander, would never let me live it down. We didn't say anything for a while. "It was his territory. You didn't stand a chance," he added after some time.

"Duly noted," I replied. We were quiet again. I finally made the turn into the parking lot of my apartment building.

"Why are we here?" Xander said, looking out the window to check my apartment building like he was checking its design.

"Where do you want to be?" I inquired, and he looked at me for a minute before he unlocked his seat belt and started to get out of the car.

"I'll get a cab," he said, but as he opened the door, the first thing he did was vomit.

"I guess that bottle didn't keep the promise of its label," I commented.

Then he started to say something, but instead, he vomited some more.

Xander

I woke up, staring at an unfamiliar ceiling. I looked around. I was in a living room.

"Good morning," Myles startled me with his sexy, hot voice.

"Why am I on your couch?" I asked.

"Because you didn't make it to my bed," he winked, and I glared at him, and Myles laughed. "You were drunk. I didn't want to take advantage of you," He moved to the other side, and I had to turn to see where he was going? It was the kitchen.

"You cook?" I asked.

"Why, do you ask? Let me guess, it's a quality you are looking for in your future boyfriend?" he was a smartass with that heart-breaking smile.

I fumed at the mention of a boyfriend.

"Here, something for your hangover," he offered me the glass, and I took it. I sipped the drink, and Myles sat beside me on the couch.

I coughed, "It's strong." It tasted like rat poison if anyone ever tasted one, other than rats.

"I'm sure it's not stronger than whatever you had last night," he sat closer, and I concentrated on finishing my rat poison drink. At this time, I didn't care if it killed me. I needed my brain to start functioning.

"Feeling better?" Myles touched my front hair, and it was the nicest feeling ever. Pushing my hair off my forehead, he was styling it with his fingers as I usually did. "Want to take a shower? I'll order you a coffee."

"Order me a coffee?" I asked.

"Sorry, not much of a cook. Lucky for us, the restaurant downstairs delivers," he took out his phone and started to order.

"Aren't you worried your boyfriend might show up? Or wait, does he even know about this apartment? Is this a place just for your hook-ups?" I inquired, and Myles only stared at me like it was the first time he had seen me. Then he chuckled.

"So, this is what the text was about?" he put the phone away and turned to face me. "You think I have a boyfriend?"

"Don't fucking lie to me, Myles. Cathy told me already. I may not meet the list for your potential boyfriend, but I sure as hell am not someone you can use to cheat on your socially approved perfect boyfriend," I started to get up, but he held my wrist and pulled me back on the couch, I landed on his lap, and his face was so close to mine.

"Do I get to say anything in my defence?" he spoke softly. There was this amusement in his eyes, and the way he looked at me was so not right for my insides. "Or I don't deserve to defend myself because I don't have a heart?" His voice sounded husky.

Okay, that was wrong of me to say that he didn't have a heart. I lowered my eyes in apology and then met his eyes again when I recalled that he was a two-timing bastard.

"What's your defence?" I questioned.

"I know you think I'm an ass who doesn't have any ethics and morals," I started to get up, and he held me in place, "but let me tell you something, I may cross all the lines when it comes to business, but one thing I'd never do is cheat in a relationship." His green eyes pierced through my soul. "Growing up, all I saw was my father cheating on my mother and my mother making this huge scene every time she found out, and then one shopping trip in Europe fixed it all. When Simon cheated on me, you know what was it that hurt me the most?" he said.

I waited.

"You." he said, and I didn't understand. "You said that I deserved it," he held my gaze.

"That's not what I meant," I defended.

"I know, but at the time you said, a pompous ass like me deserved it."

"Okay, I was wrong," I admitted, "No one deserved that," I was sorry, but I couldn't say it.

"I know you know that you were wrong. See, I believe you. So, believe me when I say I don't cheat in a relationship. I am not using you to cheat on anyone, nor am I cheating on you." He promised I stared at him dumbfounded. "So, you believe me now?" he asked with a beautiful smile as if he had reserved this smile just for me.

I was so enamoured that I could only nod in response.

He moved forward to kiss me, but I pulled back, and he looked worried as he searched my eyes.

"I need a shower," I said, and he relaxed.

"You sure do," he pressed his lips to mine anyway. "Go, take a shower. I'll order breakfast," he grabbed his phone again, and I got off from his lap and started to walk towards the bathroom. Then I stopped to turn and admire his handsome body, his piercing green eyes were focused on the phone screen.

"Want to join me in the shower?" I asked as I took my shirt off in front of him. He gazed at me as I started stripping while I continued to walk to his bathroom. I turned to look at him again and he got off the couch and took off his shirt. My eyes admired his strong muscles and taut body. He then started to take off his pants as he followed me.

I walked into the bathroom and turned on the shower. I quickly used mouthwash, and then stepped in to the shower, Myles took off his briefs when he reached the bathroom, he stood there watching me, his gaze admiring every inch of my body and I could see his dick was already becoming hard, he then stepped into the shower with me. I let the water fall on my face. Myles stepped right behind me, wrapping his arms around me, he pulled me closer. He kissed my cheek, letting the water soak our bodies, then he poured the liquid soap on his hand and rubbed it on my chest, under my arms, then down to my cock.

I rested my head back on his shoulder as the water fell on my face. Myles slightly moved and kissed my mouth. I turned around, pushing my body into his. I enjoyed our soft kiss. I felt his hands move down to my back, he grabbed my hips and pulled me closer. I wrapped my arms around him, wanting to feel his hard chest against mine. I stood on my toes to rub against his dick. He ran his long fingers between my ass crack. One of my legs moved up in reaction to give him more access. He poured more soap on his fingers and again rubbed his fingers to my ass.

When his finger breached my hole, I almost folded. Myles cleaned the soap and turned off the shower, he grabbed the towel from the shelf and dried us walking me out of the shower, then he wrapped the towel around me.

"I want you in my bed," his voice sounded raspy with need and then without a warning, he lifted me off my feet.

I gasped, "Myles."

"Don't worry I won't drop you," he assured, but I wasn't worried, or I didn't want to worry, if it was a dream I wanted to keep my eyes closed.

He gently placed me on his bed.

He then moved on top of me and kissed me, this time more desperate, just the way I knew him, he pushed his tongue inside my mouth, my body moved in reaction.

He broke our kiss and spoke in deep rough voice, "I want to fuck you."

He met my eyes and I shook my head and he looked hurt and started to pull back.

I held his arms and met his eyes, "I don't want a quick fuck, Myles. Make love to me, I want to be cherished." I demanded.

He smiled and kissed me, "I'll make love to you, Xander, like you've never been loved," he promised.

He kissed me harder, making me breathless, then he moved down to my chin, my neck. He sucked all the sensitive parts that he had now learned about my body, like the side of my neck that he sucked hard enough to make my toe curl and leave a mark. Then he moved down to my chest, kissing all the soft spots, sucking my nipples. He moved down to my stomach and ran his tongue on my navel, making my body arch in response.

He trailed his soft wet lips down to my V and kissed my shaft. Running his tongue between my slit, my hand moved to grab his hair and he met my eyes and smiled at me as he took my balls in his mouth. Then he moved down kissing me. I moved my legs up to give him more room and he ran his tongue between my cheeks. Then he held my hips and pushed them apart to run his tongue inside my hole, pushing all my boundaries, invading the tight ring. He was making me desperate.

"Myles," I whimpered with need.

He let go off my hips and moved up kissing my earlobe and letting me breathe, "You know how beautiful you look, all helpless, so desperate, on my mercy, I can do whatever I want with you," he breathed those words in my ear.

I sniggered, "that's because you are a narcissist." I teased.

"Am I?" he squeezed my balls with his giant hand.

I moaned and my body turned to the side in response.

"No," he turned me on my back so I would face him again. "I want to see your pretty face and I want you to watch when I put my cock inside you," my dick reacted with excitement.

"This anticipation is killing me." I exhaled. I didn't want to embarrass myself by coming as soon as he put his dick inside me. I wanted to enjoy this longer.

"Relax a little," he rubbed his big hand against my stomach. Making it impossible for me to relax. He smiled and grabbed the lube and condom from the side drawer.

He pushed my legs up again and my hips apart as he pushed a lubed finger inside me. My body reacted with hunger. He moved up and kissed me while his fingers continued to undo me. I wrapped my arms around him and dug my fingers inside his skin since his fingers made it impossible for me to breathe. I let go of his mouth to inhale some oxygen and he kissed down my neck. When his fingers grazed against my prostate, I whimpered with need. A few more strokes and I was on the edge.

"Oh Myles, please fuck me already," I begged in desperation.

He chuckled proudly, of course, he was Myles, and I loved that it was Myles. I met his green dilated pupil as he positioned himself between my legs.

Kneading my hips, he gradually pushed his cock slightly inside me, as he met my eyes. I felt the breach against my hole and moved to give him more access. He smiled and moved on top of me again to kiss my cheek, "Don't worry baby, I got you." he whispered. While he pushed inside me more.

My already red cheeks warmed at his use of endearment. I didn't expect him to ever call me 'baby.'

He pushed his cock further inside me, invading through the tight rings, like he was breaking down all my walls. He gradually pushed inside and out and finally hit that prostate. My body responded while I held on to him. I tried to grab my aching dick but he halted my hands, he pinned my wrists on both sides, met my eyes as he locked his fingers with mine.

"Don't touch yourself. I will make you come, Xander," he kissed me, and I groaned with need. He started fucking me for real now. I felt his desperation, his need with every stroke, while he fucked me harder hitting my prostate over and over again. He let go of my hands so he could hold me in place and that position made it harder for me to control myself, when he fucked me like that.

"Myles," I came before I could warn him, I felt my muscles squeeze around his cock and I felt him come inside me. I felt the heat of his cum as it filled the condom. He fucked me until the last drop spurt out of my dick. I watched as he pulled his dick out of me and then lay beside me. We both tried to catch our breath and he wrapped his arm around me pulling me closer, he ran his fingers on my chest and my stomach.

"I love how your skin feels, radiating, soft and warm after you come. You have this glow, like you are in the spotlight."

"Must be your side lamp," I said.

"No, it's all you, baby," he kissed my cheek and I hugged him when he pulled me closer. When I started doubting that he called me baby because he forgot my name, or he was pretending I was someone else, he added, "You are so beautiful, Xander."

I smiled and ran my lips against his wet, sweaty chest, feeling the smoothness of his skin and his soft chest hair against my lips. Myles had truely made me feel loved, even now the way he hugged me. I never wanted this moment to be over so I closed my eyes and let myself fall asleep in his arms.

Myles

"I love you," I whispered while I ran my fingers through Xander's hair, then I opened my eyes with panic and realization at what I had said, but Xander hadn't commented or reacted. I felt his steady breath against my chest and figured that he fell asleep in my arms. I exhaled with relief and slowly rolled him off me to the bed, so I wouldn't wake him. He looked so pretty and perfect and I wanted to kiss him again.

'I love you,' my own words rang in my head as if they were desperate to come out again. I shook my head and got off the bed, threw the condom in the basket and decided to take another shower.

I checked my reflection in the mirror. My cheeks were flushed, but my eyes were wild and shining, and I realized that the admission of love was not because of the awesome sex I had. I didn't just make love to Xander, I did love him. I was falling for Xander, or had already fallen.

Chapter Eleven

Feeling every word you say

.

Xander

.

I was dreading to see Dawson since I'd been ignoring all his requests to go out with him. I saw Myles at the entrance. Dawson was there as well.

"Dawson, you've already started to paint? I told you I was still working on the right shade with the suppliers, and I was going to send you the final list with colour code this afternoon," I asked Dawson.

"I'm sorry, I missed the part where you were announced my boss," Dawson retorted.

"That's not what I meant, Dawson, but I'm doing the interior," I tried to amend.

"And I have been doing this for the past seven years, think I know what I am doing," Okay, Dawson was in full attitude.

I opened my mouth to come up with some possible reply that wouldn't sound rude but put across my point.

Myles, however, beat me to it, "We don't want what's been happening for the past seven years, we need something new, and Xander is in charge of the interior, so until he gets you colour codes, order your men to stop the painting, Dawson." Myles used that Boss tone of his.

"You got it, Boss," Dawson confirmed, and Myles gave a single nod before he walked out of there, leaving me in awkward silence with Dawson.

"Dawson, if you see the shades I've worked with the suppliers for each wall, I'm sure you'll like it," I attempted to deflect the uneasy atmosphere as I opened the list on the iPad.

"Boy, can't say I saw that coming," Dawson mocked, and somehow, I knew the comment wasn't for the colour selection.

"Excuse me?"

"Of course, the corner office, expensive clothes, million-dollar project- Myles Alden. You did fucking well for your self, Xander," he sneered and gave me a stern look.

I opened my mouth to prove him wrong, but I had nothing to say, and Dawson didn't stay to listen.

I stormed out of there to find Myles. He was still in the parking lot, checking emails on his phone.

"What the fuck did you do that for? You are so full of yourself, you can't see beyond your fucking nose." I was so livid, I couldn't see straight.

"Calm the fuck down, Xander," he grabbed me from my arm and moved me to the side next to his car, so another vehicle in the parking lot could leave, which btw I hadn't noticed until then.

"What did I do?" he asked.

"What did you do? Of course, you are that fucking blind, you can't see what you did, you told Dawson that he can shove his seven years of experience up his ass and accept the paint I pick," I shouted.

"I'm pretty sure I didn't tell Dawson to shove his experience up his ass, but okay. I thought that's what you wanted," he looked genuinely confused. I was having a hard time staying mad at him.

"Yeah, but not like that, now Dawson thinks we are fucking." I said.

"But we are fucking," again with a confused expression.

"It's not ..." I tried to calm myself.

"Okay, calm down," he stroked my cheek with his cool fingers, "you need some water?"

"No," I shook my head while I tried to take a deep breath and focused on Myles' beautiful features in this bright daylight.

"So," Myles ran his fingers through my sweaty hair, "What did Dawson say?"

"It's not what he said. It's what he implied," I tried not to focus too much on his gentle hands.

"Okay, what did he imply?" he said so calmly like he had all the time in the world to listen to me.

"You know, just forget it," I tried to move, but he wouldn't let me.

"Okay, do you want me to fire him?" I felt my eyes widened. I couldn't believe, I heard him right.

"What did you say?" I asked to be sure.

"I can fire him if he is giving you so much trouble, it will be a bit inconvenient giving the timing, but I can ask HR to see if they can find a good replacement," I looked at him with open mouth, and then he smiled.

"Oh, fuck me," I turned away from him.

"Right now?" he teased.

"Shut up, Myles," I laughed.

"Hey," he grabbed me and pulled me in a hug, a gesture I hadn't expected in a million years from Myles Alden. "I know people like Dawson are bastards, he is not the first, and he is certainly not going to be the last. You are here because of who you are, and you know as well as I do that I'd have thrown your ass out the first day if I could. So, don't let people like Dawson get to you. Okay?" He pushed me back to look me in the eyes, "You'll be alright now?"

"Yeah," I nodded and kissed his lips.

He smiled, "kissing your boss in public, think about your reputation, Xander."

"Enough now," I laughed, and he kissed my cheek.

"Okay, got a meeting with my dad at the head office, so I'll see you tonight?"

"Yeah," I watched him drive away.

Myles

I sat through the meeting with board members. Discussed new projects. Talked about progress on current projects. I zoned in and out of the meeting. My mind kept going back to Xander.

Things were not so casual anymore. I said, 'I love you' even if Xander didn't hear it, I couldn't take those words back. Okay, Xander didn't fit into my perfect boyfriend's profile but was that all that mattered. Sure, Xander didn't belong to a big name family. Being with Xander didn't help me make any contacts in the business. Business magazines and bloggers would have a hell of a time digging dirt into Xander's background, and I was afraid they wouldn't find anything acceptable. Dad wouldn't be pleased. Okay, but with all those cons, why was I still thinking of asking Xander on a real date? Why the sex wasn't enough? Anything with Xander was never enough.

"You seemed distracted," Dad asked after the meeting at his office.

"Yeah, I was just thinking about the project," I deflected.

"So, how's it coming?" he questioned.

"Making good progress should be ready in time."

"How's the new kid doing? What's his face?" he asked.

"Alexander."

"Yes, Alexander. Does he know what he is doing?"

"Yeah, he's very talented. You've seen him at your anniversary. He was very creative." I couldn't help but smile, thinking of Xander, "Also, the new designs he presented are impressive, the construction is almost done, and he already started on paints. I think the model home will be ready next week."

"Hmm, interesting, what about Simon?"

"Simon?"

"Yes, he'd be joining us soon. He said he already spoke to you."

"Oh yes, slipped out of my mind. He is joining next week."

"Simon is a good kid," I knew what Dad meant, but I nodded, I didn't want this conversation with Dad.

"I've got some meetings. I'll head out now," I stood up to leave.

"Yes, sure, I'll come to visit the model home," he said as I left his office.

My phone pinged with a text message from Xander. "Sorry, can't come right now, something urgent came up. I'll see you tomorrow."

I called Xander immediately.

"Myles, can't talk right now," there was a lot of noise behind him. "You can't make phone calls," someone said. "Xander is not part of it," someone else said, "we have a warrant to search the entire house, no phones," another person said, and the phone got disconnected.

My phone pinged with a text message from Xander. "Sorry, can't come right now, something urgent came up. I'll see you tomorrow."

I reached Xander's place as soon as I could. "Xander," he was standing outside of his house with a couple more guys.

"Myles," he came to me.

"Oh, thank God, you are okay." I hugged him. Thousands of scenarios had run through my brain the time it took me to get here. Seeing him all right was a relief. "What happened?" I asked.

"The cops are searching our home," he said casually as if it was a routine.

"What?" I didn't understand. I'd never heard cops ever searching the home of anyone I knew. "What are they searching?"

"Uncle Luca brewed rum in his apartment and tried to sell it without a licence."

"Allegedly," the other guy standing next to Xander said.

"Yeah, allegedly," Xander smirked.

"So, you are being searched because your uncle did something illegal?" that didn't make any sense.

"No, Uncle Luca is not my real uncle." he seemed calm and smiled.

"He's everyone's uncle," the guy again interfered.

"I'm renting one of the rooms in this house with Uncle Luca, Thomas, and Larry."

"What's up," Larry waved. Thomas was the guy who kept interrupting.

"But it's not fair to you," I was genuinely concerned.

Both Thomas and Larry laughed.

"In this side of town, everything is fair, Myles."

One of the constables came and announced something to the tenants in incoherent words.

"Great," Xander said.

"What?" I asked.

"House is sealed," Thomas answered.

"I'm going to Papas. You're coming too, Xander?" Larry asked.

"Maybe later," Xander replied.

"Why would you be going to his Papa's house?"

"No, Papas is like a lounge."

"You are not staying at a lounge. You are coming with me." I started to walk to my car when I noticed he didn't follow me, so I stopped and turned to face him. "Well, what are you waiting for?" I asked, and he smiled then followed me.

Xander

I wasn't sure what to make of it. What was it between us? I was scared to admit that Myles actually cared for me. He wouldn't show up at my place if he didn't care. To be honest, I was so afraid to open my eyes and face reality. I wanted to live in this dream a little longer, where Myles cared for me.

"You are awake," Myles whispered in my ear, his warm body touched my back, and I moved closer to be in his arms. And Myles pulled me in the safety of his arms. He kissed my cheeks, "open your eyes," he used that bedroom voice that just melted me. I opened my eyes to meet the green gems in his eyes. I traced his face with my hand. He was so beautiful, so perfect, he kissed my palm, and it seemed so much like we were in a relationship. The realization worried me, but I wanted to stay in this dream. Myles kissed me softly like he wanted to memorize the taste and texture of my lips, and I wanted to savour his every kiss.

Myles

I greeted Dad at the housing site, "not much snow this season, can't say I hate it" I unlocked the door to the model home.

"Where is everyone? Aren't they preparing for the event?" Dad asked.

"Some are at the back. Rest, I gave the morning off. I thought I'd give you an exclusive tour."

Dad smiled in response, but he wasn't happy.

"Nice," was the first thing he said about the living room.

"Isn't it? When Xander mentioned how it would give that open space look and the impact the painting would have, I wasn't convinced.

I could hardly visualize it, but now I see it, and it's beautiful." I just stared at the large painting on the living room wall matching with the paint in the room, giving it that wintery yet homey feel.

"Hmm," that's all the response I got from dad, and he moved to check the kitchen.

"All the appliances are from Michaels. They are giving us the 50% rebate they promised last year."

"What is this?" he pressed on the tap in the corner, and it emitted gas. He jumped.

"Oh, it's like a mini bar, soda water basically," I readjusted the pipe on the tap.

"That's a good idea," Dad appreciated.

"Yeah, Xander wanted to have a unique feature in the kitchen that's both in demand and not part of every household. Xander is very creative." I smiled.

"Hmm," again, that's all the response I got.

The bedroom, gaming room, kids' room were all equally impressive.

We finally finished our tour and returned to the living room. Dad stood in front of the painting and silently stared at it.

"Is this an original?" he finally spoke again.

"No, it's a replica of Ethreno's painting," I informed.

"Hmm, isn't it something? The painter did a great job of fooling everyone, but the paint is not the same, only if you watch closely you can tell its cheapness," he smirked.

I didn't say anything, knowing my dad, the comment wasn't about the painting, and I wasn't interested in listening to his analogies.

Xander

It started to snow when I reached the site. The model home was finally ready for me to start on the Christmas theme. I just had to wait for photographers to collect all the images, and then I could start decorating the house for Christmas. I noticed Myles' car on the site and smiled involuntarily. I parked the car under the shade in case it started to snow more, and then I made my way to the model home.

I entered the house when I heard someone talking. Myles was with someone, maybe a client. I didn't want to disturb them. I started to move back when I heard my name, and curiosity got the best of me.

"When I met him at the anniversary, I suspected this would happen. He is certainly a type," I heard Mr. Edwin Alden, Myles' dad speak.

"Xander is nothing like Simon, Dad," Myles said.

"Of course he isn't. Simon is Barrister Morgan's son, he has inherited wealth and education, and is certainly the type of boyfriend you can bring home," the words stung like a bitter truth.

"Dad, I'm not dating Simon anymore," Myles said.

"It doesn't have to be forever. Simon told me he's very sorry for what he did to you. If he could erase that day from his life, he would."

"That doesn't change the fact that Simon has someone else in his life now," Myles said, and I couldn't help but think that the only reason Simon and Myles were not together today was because Simon was dating someone else.

"Not anymore," Mr. Alden announced.

"What? How? What happened?" Myles asked.

"Why don't you call Simon and find out," Mr. Alden said.

"Dad, if Simon wants to talk to me, he will call."

"Of course, it's your life, but let me give you a piece of advice I wish my father had given me, you will meet two types of women, or in your case men, the one you can keep at home and the other you can take to bed. I don't think I have to tell you which type your designer falls into," that was enough for me to hear. I doubled-back and left the house.

Chapter Twelve

It would have been easy to hate you.

.

Xander

.

The problem wasn't that Mr. Alden had defined my type as a cheap floozy, the problem was that truth hurt. The night of Simon's birthday when Myles had called me on my shit, I had done precisely what he said. I'd again spent that night with Ryan. And it wasn't just that I was so blind that I kept falling for my cheater ex, but it was the fact that Ryan had paid my rent from time to time. Yes, I wanted to give it so many names than to admit that I had whored myself for rent money. Mr. Alden was also right, I didn't even compare to Simon. He was a Barrister's son. I was born on the cheap side of the town, my mom worked as a maid at a five-star hotel and was a drug addict. As for my father, my mother didn't know who he was, and she died long before I could ask her anything.

I only got to meet Simon because his family was mad at him, and he had been thrown out of the house for being gay. I had posted an ad for a roommate because I couldn't afford to pay my rent. I was barely managing my college tuition fee with all the night jobs I was doing at the bar. Simon was so sweet and innocent. He didn't understand how the world worked. He didn't know why I let Ryan cheat on me and kept going back to him. Other than cheating, Ryan wasn't bad, he kept me safe and always looked out for me. The neighbourhoods I grew up in were anything but safe, but no one would dare touch me since they all knew I was Ryan's boyfriend.

Simon didn't understand any of that. Simon became like this little brother I never had, and I felt like protecting him from this ugly world, so when Myles entered Simon's life, I felt a bit overprotective and may have judged Myles with the only microscope I was familiar with. I didn't even consider that I didn't stand anywhere in the status equation that Myles Alden and Simon Morgan shared. And today, I was shown a mirror.

How did I forget that I was nothing more to Myles Alden than a cheap hookup? No matter how good and secure it felt in Myles' arms. It was all a delusion. Myles would never accept me in public, he made it very clear that first night that I didn't have the potential to be his perfect boyfriend. And I still dared to dream of it. I dared to fall for him. It would have been easier if I still hated him.

I didn't answer any of Myles' calls that day and avoided running into him at the office.

"Hey Xander," Simon cheered as I was about to leave the office.

"Simon," I hugged him and immediately felt guilty like I'd been cheating on him, stealing something that was rightfully Simon's.

"Look at you, all dressed up," he looked genuinely happy to see me, and I felt like a liar.

"Yeah, the office code," of course the fancy suit didn't really hide what I was.

"We'd be working at the same office," Simon grinned.

"I know, I heard. Congratulations, and welcome," I smiled.

"Thank you, it feels like we are in college again," we laughed together at some of the memories we shared. Even though we didn't really go to the same college, we spent most days at cafes and doing our homework together.

"Xander," Myles called from behind. When our eyes met, I immediately looked away and focused on Simon.

"Myles," Simon gave Myles his best smile.

"Simon, you are starting today?" he asked.

"Yeah, I'm really excited. Dad said I'm lucky to be Mr. Chin's assistant, apparently, he's the best." Simon looked excited.

"He sure is," Myles confirmed.

"Oh, Myles, I wanted to talk if you have time," Simon asked Myles.

"Aa yeah, sure," he said to Simon while he tried to hold my gaze but I looked away.

"Simon, I have to go. I'll see you later okay," I gave him a quick hug, without another glance towards Myles.

I left for the site. I had only one day to the event, there wasn't really any time to cry over a heartbreak.

Myles

"You like it here so far?" I tried to converse with Simon, even though my mind was occupied with this unnerving feeling that something wasn't right with Xander.

"I love it. Mr. Chin is very nice and gives very detailed notes. And a bit of a perfectionist."

"Of course, we only hire the best."

"You sure do. I'm so glad to see Xander working here."

"Yeah, he is very talented," I smiled.

"I thought you guys hated each other."

"Yeah, we kind of did, I guess. But Xander is smart, and no one deserves this job better than him."

"Does he now?"

"Sure, we only hire the best," I boasted.

"You're praising Xander now, that is something," Simon laughed.

"Simon, am I glad to see you," Dad interrupted. I was surprised to see him here. He hardly stepped out of the head office, let alone visit my branch.

"Hello, Mr. Alden. Thank you so much for this opportunity."

"You've earned it, boy. How's your old man recovering?"

"He is good, recovering fine," Simon smiled.

"Simon, you didn't tell me your dad was sick?" I asked.

"It's nothing. He's fine. Just had an angioplasty so had to stay at the hospital for a couple of days."

"You know you can call me at any time. We are still friends," I meant what I said.

"Of course, thank you, Myles." He gave me a quick hug.

"Tell your old man I want to see him on the golf course again."

"Yes, I will. Dad will be happy to hear it. Okay, I will leave you two to talk," Simon replied and walked towards Mr. Chin's office.

"Isn't he a nice boy," Dad said as he took a seat at my office.

"Yes, Dad, Simon is nice. Is that the reason why you came?"

"To see Simon?" he gave me a quizzical look. "Why would you think that?"

"Dad, Simon and I are not together. We probably should have never been together from the start. I'm telling you this because I don't want you to get your hopes up." I couldn't play this mind game with Dad anymore.

He laughed, "I only hope best for you, Myles."

"Then, best for me is not Simon." I had to be upfront with Dad.

"So, it's Alexander?" he asked like he was daring me.

I could feel my cheeks heat, "maybe, yes, I mean yes, Dad. It's Xander." There I said it. Dad always made me feel nervous. And like an idiot, I sought his approval when I knew he would never be happy with anything I did that he hadn't planned, like the time I came out to him, I felt so nervous around him because I wanted him to accept me. He didn't outright reject me, but the only time I saw acceptance in his eyes was when I met Simon at one of his parties. Maybe that is why I asked Simon out on a date.

"And how does Xander feel about this?" that question took me by surprise. How could Dad know Xander and I didn't have any offical discussion about the relationship yet.

"I don't know Dad, I'm pretty sure he likes me." I know the answer didn't sound confident.

"There is a reason why I said to you what I did. Alexander is not the one for your home, son."

I stopped myself from rolling my eyes.

"Dad, please don't start with that. I am not like you. I am certainly not a cheater, there is only one for me." I couldn't believe where I got this confidence from, maybe because I hadn't been more certain in my life than I was about Xander.

"And that's Alexander?" he raised his eyebrow.

"Yes, it's Alexander, Dad," I confirmed once again.

"I wish it didn't come to this," he said, taking an envelope out of his pocket and gave it to me.

"What is it?" I was starting to get worried.

"You may open it," he said.

I huffed and opened the envelope. There were a couple of pictures of Xander and me in not so decent kissing.

"Dad, you've spied on me?" I fumed.

"Certainly not. What do I have to gain from it? This is your Alexander's doing, he sent me those pictures."

"What?" I didn't believe it. "Why would Xander send you these pictures?" I questioned.

"The only reason a boy like Alexander would sleep with his boss." I just stared at him. "Money, son, this is all for money."

"Money? Xander sent you these for Money?" It didn't make any sense to me. This was not Xander, and I certainly didn't trust my father.

"Yes, he's blackmailing me that he will charge you with workplace harassment if I don't pay him what he wants," Dad said.

"No, Dad. Xander is not like that," I insisted.

"Why is it so hard to believe that a boy from the lower town hustled you for money?" Dad's words pierced through my heart like an ugly reality and everything froze in place, and the pictures fell from my hand. "I'm sorry, Myles, but there is a reason why boys like that should never be welcomed in our homes," he added.

Xander hustled me? My heart started to sink.

"I only wanted to tell you the reality of this Alexander, rest is up to you. I'll see you at the open house." Dad started to leave.

"How much money did he ask for?" My voice was barely above a whisper.

Dad paused at the door and turned to face me, "Half a million," then he left.

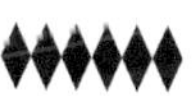

Xander

The model home was open for those who booked an appointment with a realtor. Other than that, I had the place to myself, and my event planning team.

"Where do you want it?" Ryan asked, carrying the bulky tree.

"Right there on the cross," I'd made a cross with red tape on the floor.

"Like I can see the cross behind this bush," I laughed at Ryan's frustration. The tree was too big. Even a big guy like Ryan couldn't see beyond it.

I held the tree from the other side and helped him keep it on the cross I had made for its spot. It was in the perfect center of the living room.

"So, this is the house? It's nice. How much is it?"

"Three million or so," I replied.

He whistled, "I'd never be able to afford it." I placed a border around the tree, so there were no accidents. "But *you* may be, with that rich boyfriend of yours," he winked.

"He's not my boyfriend, Ryan," I tried to busy myself with decorating the ornaments to avoid feeling anything.

"Why not? I thought he liked you. He was ready to fight me for you."

"A guy like me is never a boyfriend to a rich guy like him."

"What are you talking about? Why not? There is nothing wrong with you. You are perfect, Xander." Ryan encouraged, and I couldn't help but smile.

"Thanks. Can you help me unload more stuff?"

"Sure."

We went outside to get more decorations from the trailer.

"And who's picking Mrs. Cook?" I asked.

"I think Thomas," he said.

"You think? Just confirm it, will you?" I scowled at him.

"Okay, boss." Ryan made me laugh again. Ryan and I grew up together and I knew I could always count on him. He may be an awful boyfriend but he was a good friend.

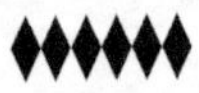

Myles

I sat in my car watching Xander flirting with his ex. Ryan. Was he really an ex? I laughed at myself.

I came to confront Xander because part of me still didn't want to believe what was right in front of me.

This wasn't the first time, of course. A snake couldn't change his nature.

Chapter Thirteen

Only, if I didn't love you.

.

Xander

.

"Glen, plug in the lights now." The house came to life with dazzling colourful lights.

"This is so beautiful, Xander." Mrs. Cook applauded. "I've never seen anything like it," the lights reflected in her eyes.

"Thank you, Mrs. Cook, this event wouldn't be possible without your help," Mrs. Cook and the boys had set up little Christmas shops around the garden to give it an authentic small-town Christmas market look.

"You'd do just fine without me, dear. It's you who did us a favour and included us in your event," she smiled kindly.

"Maybe because I'm selfish, I learned on Mr. and Mrs. Alden's anniversary, that I can only count on the people I know and trust. Plus, I owe you for the band."

"Hush, you paid us with the leftover food from the event. Those caterers were very sweet."

"Oh yeah, I have them today too. If you want to go say hi, they are at the back," the temporary kitchen was arranged at the other side of the garden near the dinner tables.

"Oh, I'll stay here, keep an eye on the boys. It looks like your guests have started arriving."

The cars had started coming in. I wanted to feel excited, this was my first big event and the first house I decorated, but still, something was missing. I hadn't seen Myles since yesterday. He didn't even call me after meeting Simon at the office. Did he believe what his father said? He didn't object, so maybe yes.

I started to welcome all the guests at the entrance. "Alexander," Mrs. Alden came and hugged me. "This is a work of art. You are a brilliant artist, Alexander."

"Thank you, Mrs. Alden." I was amazed at how warm she had become towards me.

"I tell my husband you are a keeper, right, Edwin." She turned to Mr. Alden.

"Of course, Alexander is very skillful indeed." Mr. Alden said.

"See, what did I say?" Mrs. Alden said. "oh, look at those little Christmas stalls. Is that a Christmas market? Oh my goodness," Mrs. Alden didn't let me answer and walked in the direction of those Christmas stalls as if she were mesmerized. I smiled at her enthusiasm.

"My wife is very fond of you, Alexander," Mr. Alden said.

"I'm grateful, Sir." I smiled.

Mr. Alden didn't return my smile. "Of course, I appreciate how talented you are. Not everyone has the talent to sleep with their boss within a month of their new job," this time he smiled with sternness in his eyes. "Your contract will be over after tonight's event. Unfortunately, my business doesn't need your talent, you shouldn't have any trouble finding another job," he touched my shoulder as he smiled and walked to the house, leaving me to feel awful about myself.

"Xander, a photographer, wants you to pose for a picture with the house," Glen interrupted my self-pity.

"Yeah, in a minute," I said. I just had to get through this night. I braced myself.

"You are okay?" Ryan came and asked.

"Yeah, wow, you look good in the suit." It was the first time I saw him in a suit.

"Had to rent it, cost me a fortune. What's the need of a valet wearing a suit?"

"You'll be compensated, and you are not just a valet, you are also going to make sure no one gets behind the wheel after drinking. And be a silent spy. Let me know if something goes wrong." I instructed.

"You got it, boss."

"And stop calling me that," I warned.

"Yes, boss." He winked when I glared at him.

I laughed with Ryan, but then he went silent. I followed his glare to see what caught his attention and made him frown.

It was Myles with Simon. Myles had opened the passenger door for Simon and held his hand as they walked to the entrance. My eyes zeroed on their locked hands together.

"Xander," Simon hugged me. I forced myself to smile. Myles stood beside Simon and looked me straight in the eyes with that proud smile. "This is so beautiful, Xander. I feel like I want to buy this house," Simon gaped at the house with awe.

"I'm sure Myles would give you a good price," I remarked.

"Of course, anything for Simon, especially if we decide to live together in this house." He wrapped his arm around Simon, and I was having trouble looking away from that.

"What's Ryan doing here?" Simon pointed in Ryan's direction, who was now helping guests park their car.

"I needed people I could trust. Unfortunately, not everyone meets that criteria in the opulent side of this town." I looked up at Myles.

Myles smirked, "trust? Really? Is that a new drug in your impoverished side of town?"

"Myles," Simon warned him, just like old times.

"Sorry, Simon, I'm a bit behind on street slang. Better we stick to our opulent side of the town." he glowered at me. "Come on. I'll give you a tour of the house." he held Simon's hand as he walked him to the model home.

"Glen, can you watch the entrance? I need a little break." I radioed Glen, so I didn't end up crying in front of the photographers.

I walked to one of the empty rooms and closed the door behind me and tried to calm my tears that were threatening to fall.

Myles

The event was well put together. The little stalls were amazing. Every guest loved it. Simon had many of those hand made cookies with little ornaments and Christmas tree designs on them. Mrs. Cook said she and her boys had baked those cookies. Also, the paintings and sculptures the boys from Mrs. Cook's group home had made were really nice.

At first, I thought Xander had approached some charity for the event, but then I learned from Mrs. Cook that Xander is one of her boys. He was raised in her group home. She told me all the things Xander had done for the boys and how he had spent most of his income to help Mrs. Cook's group home. Mrs. Cook couldn't stop praising Xander.

"Simon, I am just going to the house for a minute. I'll be back okay," I told Simon, who didn't seem to need me because he was busy getting his arms painted at one of the stalls.

Xander and Dawson were giving an official tour of the house when I found Xander.

"This room can be your gaming room, your study room, your workout place, or a lady's cave. Seriously, who gave men the right to decide women do not need alone time?" Xander said, and all the women in the room cheered. Then his smile faded as his eyes met mine, and he stopped for a second before resuming, "I have made different catalogues, you may find at the entrance. We can customize it however you like it."

"Even if you like to remove any unwanted walls, we can look at it. Have a vision, share with us," Dawson added, and they all started to leave for the other room of the house.

Before Xander left the room, I grabbed his arm and pulled him back, meeting his wide eyes. Then I turned and met Dawson's eyes as I locked the door behind him.

"What are you doing, Myles? I have a tour to finish."

"Dawson can do it," I turned to face him again. He looked so gorgeous, I had to question him. Why did he do it? Blackmail me? Did he need money? Was this all part of a sick plan? I had so many questions, but as I stared into his beautiful light eyes, temptation took over, I moved forward and pressed my lips to his. For a second, he let me, then he pulled away.

"I'm not..."

"You are not what?"

"I'm not your fucking whore, Myles," I could see the tears glistening in his eyes, and it burned my insides. "I know what you think of me. I know what your Dad said."

So, it was true? "Of course," I punched the wall.

"What are you doing?" he exclaimed.

"I should have known. I still didn't want to believe it. No matter how nicely you dress, you'll still be that filthy pest from the lower town." Xander kicked my leg. "Fuck," making me bend, he grabbed my collar.

"What did you call me?" he questioned.

I grabbed his arm, spun us and pinned him against the door. "I said you are a filthy little pest," he tried to hit me again, but I pushed his legs with mine, holding him in place.

"What the fuck are you doing, Myles?"

"You are trying to hit me. I am just stopping you," his face was just an inch from mine, and I was losing my mind. I missed him so much these past few days and my body was craving him.

"Because you're an asshole," he whispered.

"And what are you? A hustler? A blackmailer? Does being born on the wrong side of the town justify it all? Is it fair, what you did to me?"

"Fuck off, I didn't do anything to you," he shoved me, and I let him.

"You don't remember Xander, but I do. This is not the first time you pulled a fast one on me. But this time, you really crossed the line. You say I don't have a heart?" I grabbed his collar, "did you bother to look inside your self? I bet a crucial piece is missing, and that's your soul," I took out the cheque I had written for him, "you sold it for half a million dollars?" I threw the cheque on his face and let go of him. He stared at me with his wide hazel eyes. Then he gradually picked the cheque from the floor.

"I asked you for half a million?" he acted surprised but I wasn't buying it, not this time.

"You don't ask, Xander, because if you did, I wouldn't have cared, but you blackmailed. Once a hustler, always a hustler, right?"

He just stared at me, "What are you on?"

I laughed, "You and your games."

He looked at the cheque again.

"What? Is this not enough? You want more?" I asked.

"I told you," he ripped the cheque, "I'm not your fucking whore," he threw the little pieces of that cheque in my face. "You can't buy me."

"Xander," I grabbed his wrist and stopped him in place.

"You think you can pay me, and marry Simon, since he meets your potential fucking perfect boyfriend list, then you can keep me on the side for your bed? And then accuse me of hustling you? Seriously? Let me tell you, Myles Alden, When I'll hustle you, you won't see it coming."

I just stared at him in disbelief. "Wait, you just ripped the half-million dollars cheque."

"I'm gong to fucking rip you too, if you don't get out of my way, Myles," He started to leave again. I grabbed his hand and stopped him.

"Xander, wait, did you meet my dad?"

"What kind of a fucking question is that? Of course, I met your dad, he just told me his company doesn't need my talent anymore and I can find another job."

"What?" It didn't make any sense.

"He just fired me. Didn't he include you in the memo?"

I just stared at him.

"Just now? So, you didn't meet him, and you didn't send him any pictures?"

"What pictures? What the fuck are you talking about? Are you on drugs?" Xander was mad, and he looked maddening as hell. I smiled at the revelation. I knew I shouldn't have trusted dad.

"But, then why were you mad at me? You didn't return my calls," it still confused me, Xander had stopped answering my calls.

"You think you have any right to ask me a question? What the fuck are you doing here with Simon?"

"Oh Simon. Shit," I had asked Simon as my date to the event because I was so mad at Xander and I knew it would hurt him. "Xander," I started to explain myself but he pulled away and unlocked the door to leave.

"Xander," I called after him. He stopped but not because of me. Simon stood in front of him at the door.

"Xander, Myles, what are you guys doing here?" Simon asked.

"Simon, we were just discussing..." Xander started to say.

"Oh, shut the front door," Simon exclaimed and we both went silent.

"Xander is that guy?" Simon asked me. "My best friend? Oh my God," Simon looked at Xander.

"Simon, listen." I started to say.

"Listen? What can you possibly say?" Simon inquired, and Xander and I looked at each other, "Oh my God, now you are talking with your eyes?"

Few other people in the house were trying to listen so, Xander again closed the door.

"You were doing this behind my back," Simon accused.

"No," Xander said. And I just looked at him, and then Simon looked at me.

"Not when we were dating," I defended.

"Oh so, right when we broke off, you two thought it was okay to date behind my back?"

"We are not dating," we both said at the same time.

"You are not? So, what are you doing?"

We both didn't answer.

"Unbelievable," Simon yelped, and Glen's voice came on Xander's radio asking for him to come to stage.

"Simon, I have to go, but trust me, our intention was never to hurt you. I'll have to explain later," Xander rushed out the door, leaving me with Simon.

"I know Xander, he'd never intentionally hurt me but you, why did you ask me on a date today?" Simon glared at me.

"That was wrong of me. I am so sorry," I apologized.

"You are sorry? Did you ever care about me, Myles?" Simon asked.

"Of course. I still care about you, Simon."

"Oh yeah? Okay, so tell me this, what's my favourite food?"

I didn't know what this had to do with proving that I cared, but I answered.

"Ah, you like Chinese." I shrugged.

"It's Italian. Chinese is Xander's favourite food, but you already knew that, didn't you?" he said.

I opened my mouth, and Simon interrupted with another question, "Okay, what's my favourite colour?"

"You never told me that." I was pretty sure.

"Okay, what's Xander's favourite colour?"

Blue. I knew it. Xander had somehow incorporated it in every corner of the house. I didn't say it, though; I just stared at Simon, and he knew. Simon laughed without humour.

"It doesn't mean I didn't care about you, Simon. And I never cheated on you." I insisted.

"Okay, you cared about me? What's my favourite vacation destination?"

"I know that one, Rome," I said with confidence.

"Scotland," he corrected. "Rome is where Xander wants to visit."

"What's my biggest fear?"

"Heights?" I guessed.

"Public speaking. I told you so many times the worst part about being a lawyer was public speaking, but it also helped me overcome my fear. Were you ever listening?" I just stared at him because I had nothing to say for myself. "I bet you know what's Xander's biggest fear."

"Horror movies," I muttered.

"Bingo."

I was so done. "You are a fucking good lawyer, you know that?" I said, and Simon laughed again shaking his head.

"I'd been feeling guilty all this time for cheating on you. I bet if you met Xander first, you wouldn't even have looked at me. So, don't ever say you didn't cheat on me, okay. Now we are even, Myles," he walked away before I could say anything in my defence.

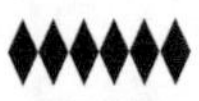

Myles

I found Xander on the stage with Dawson announcing the winners of the draw. I stepped onto the stage and walked straight to Xander. Both Xander and Dawson fell silent.

"What is it, Myles?" he whispered away from the mic.

"I want to talk to you."

"Maybe later, we are just finishing up," Xander whispered again.

I moved next to the mic so everyone could hear me, but I faced Xander as I spoke, "I want to say it here, Xander, so that you don't have any doubts about my intentions. And no one else could manipulate us anymore."

"What are you talking about? Get off the stage, Myles," Xander stepped closer and whispered.

"No, let everyone hear it. You know how you always taunt me and yes, I accept that you don't meet the requirement of my socially accepted perfect boyfriend, the one my father would approve of, but you are perfect for me, and that's all that matters to me now. You matter to me Xander, and I don't care if anyone else has a problem with what we do, as long as you say, it's okay, and you want me just as much as I want you." I announced holding his gaze.

.

Xander

.

My cheeks burned at Myles' public declaration of his desire for me. I looked at the people and all eyes were on us, while they sat on the edge of their seats to listen. I grabbed Myles' hand and walked him off the stage. Everyone's eyes were still following us.

"What the fuck did you do that for?" I stopped and faced Myles.

"I wanted you to trust me," Myles replied.

"And what made you think that if we didn't have this conversation in front of a crowd, I wouldn't trust you?" I scolded.

"Maybe because all you ever did is judge me. Why else would you accuse me of treating you like a whore?" he said.

"Lower your volume," I warned, and he just laughed.

"What?" I asked.

Myles moved forward and placed a kiss on my lips. "You know, how adorable you look when you are bossy."

I couldn't help but smile.

He kissed me again in front of everyone. Few people cheered, including Ryan, and the photographers started clicking our pictures. I watched Mr. Edwin Alden leave the event.

"I think we should go on a real date sometime," Myles said.

"Took you long enough to say that," I chided.

"Ooo Kay, so, maybe I should not delay on this one." he took out a key and gave me.

"What is it?" I asked.

"This's my apartment key. I wanted you to have it since the first time you came to my apartment."

"You what?" I was having a hard time believing all of it.

"Yes, Xander, I wanted you since forever. It's just taken me this long to realize. I don't want to waste any more time. I want you to move in with me."

I stopped caring about who was watching and kissed Myles just like I wanted to.

"What about Simon?" I worried for Simon. I never wanted to hurt him.

"He is fine. He kind of helped me realize that-"

"Realize what?"

"That I am in love with you," he held my gaze as if he didn't want to miss my reaction.

"I think, I..." I moved closer, my eyes fixed on his lips, and my hands rested on his chest, enjoying the feeling of Myles being mine.

"You what?" he prompted.

"I am in love with you too," I raised my eyes to meet his enamoured eyes. And I couldn't believe I was this fortunate to have earned such love from Myles.

He kissed me again, and I allowed myself to be lost in him.

Epilogue

Before you, Christmas was never this perfect

.

Myles

.

"Where are you going?" I pulled Xander in my arms when he tried to get out of bed.

"To get ready, it's seven o'clock."

"I thought my dad fired you," I mumbled, spooning him.

"Thanks for that early morning reminder, but your office is not where I want to be today. Tomorrow is Christmas, and I made a promise to Mrs. Cook that I would help decorate, but since I am late, the boys already took care of it, so I am going to help her with baking and cooking," he kissed me and rolled out of my arms.

I groaned at him, missing his warmth.

"Okay, I will come with you," I got out of the bed and watched him give me an eyeful.

"What did you say?" he asked.

I chuckled. "If you were not busy checking me out, you would have heard me," I stepped into the bathroom, turned on the water and started brushing my teeth. He came and wrapped his arms around me.

"I am allowed to check you out, you are mine," he met my eyes in the mirror, I cleaned my mouth and turned to face him.

"As long as you are mine," I kissed his mouth.

"I'm yours," he promised, and I wanted to ask him to promise that he was mine forever, but when he deepened our kiss, I got lost in him.

His phone rang interrupting us.

"It's a text from Ryan, they are already there, I have to go," he quickly brushed his teeth and moved towards the shower.

"I am coming with you, lets take the shower together," I said grabbing his hand and pulling him under shower.

"It's cold," Xander complained.

"It's because you are hot," I commented, and he laughed.

"I meant you are literally hot, because you are desperate for me to fuck you," I pushed my dick between his legs.

"Am I? Maybe I want to fuck you," he said meeting my eyes.

I smiled, "Is that what you want?"

He completely turned to face me and placed his arms around me.

"Maybe not right now, but want to know if it is a possibility."

I kissed his sweet lips, "If this is what you want, we can do it," I was ready to give anything to Xander.

"Not if you don't want it," he searched my eyes. "Have you tried it?"

"I tried it. I didn't like it, but it was a long time ago, if this is what you like, we can try it."

"Seriously?" he scrutinized at me.

"Everything is better with you, Xander. Even if I won't like it, I'll still get pleasure of watching you come inside me."

He just stared at me in disbelief and I kissed him.

"I love you," I said and ran my hand down his cock.

"Umm," he moved forward and hugged me, "I love you, too," he said.

I could never get over hearing him say that he loved me. I grabbed his hips and pulled him closer.

I turned off the tap and we stepped out of the shower. I helped him dry. Admiring his beautiful golden skin, I sucked the hollow of his neck and loved the way his body reacted.

"You know, the first time I saw you, I thought I could never have you, you were so out of my reach, but I wanted you so desperately."

"You wanted me when you were with Simon?" He glared at me.

"No, I mean. I don't know." I couldn't deny it. I didn't know I wanted him when I was with Simon, even if I never admitted before, but Simon's interrogation the other day made me realize I always wanted Xander. "I am talking about the first time I met you, at that club. You seriously don't remember?" I searched his eyes in hopes that he did, that I had made some kind of impact in his life as he had made in mine.

"You are saying, we met before? Like before Simon? How is that possible? I'd remember," he looked worried.

I laughed it off. "It's okay," I ran my fingers through his hair. "It was a long time ago."

"Okay, then, tell me about it," he urged, keeping his head on my shoulder.

"It was my graduation night and I went to the lower town club with my friends for something new and forbidden, that's where I met you. And you did fit the profile of forbidden, I couldn't take my eyes off you. You were so beautiful. When you asked me to dance, I felt like the luckiest man alive and when you kissed me, I was in heaven," I ran my hand on his back, feeling his smooth skin.

"I kissed you? Why don't I remember?" he asked, searching my eyes.

"You took some drugs, maybe because of that, or you didn't think I was important enough to remember."

"It's not possible, you are so hot," he smiled then he lowered his eyes. "I had some memory laps in the past because of drugs."

"I figured," I kissed his forehead.

"What did we do, after we kissed?"

I laughed, "you don't wanna know?"

"Why? Was it that bad?"

I kissed him taking away all his worries.

"No, it was just, as it was meant to be."

"We never met after that because I didn't remember? Is that why you hated me?"

"I don't think I ever hated you, but yeah, I told myself that I did," I admitted.

"And you couldn't tell me that because of Simon," he concluded.

I shook my head. "No, I had too much of an ego to ever confess how you made me feel."

He just stared in surprise and I kissed him, "aren't we getting late?" I reminded.

"Oh fuck, we gotta run." Xander ran out of the bathroom all naked and I followed.

"Don't touch that," I took the green frosting bottle from a kid who looked five at most. And he showed me his green tongue in protest. Whoever said kids were adorable, they must be selling you something.

While I was dealing with this green monster, the other kid stole the white frosting.

"Don't. We don't eat frosting. It's for the cookies. And get off the kitchen island." I picked the child from the kitchen island and kept him on the floor. Then three kids started arguing with me at once and another stole the red frosting.

"Xander!" I called but he didn't hear me, he was out fixing the lights that these kids had broken.

"Oh fuck," The fire alarm went off when the oven started burning. I took out the cookies' tray.

Then finally Xander came running.

"They are all burned, you didn't take them out?" Xander complained, fanning the alarm.

"The timer didn't go off," I showed him that small white timer that was still ticking.

"You've set it for an hour, we only needed eighteen minutes," Xander exclaimed.

"I've set it for eighteen minutes. This fucking thing is broken," I complained and he glared at me. "Sorry," I added, realizing there were kids watching us intently.

"Myles, it's okay, we'll make more," he said and started gathering ingredients. "What happened to frosting?"

"The kids ate it." I told.

"You let the kids eat frosting?"

"I didn't let anyone do anything, they are f…" I stopped and looked around then whispered my thought, "they are little thieves."

He laughed, "we have to make frosting too."

"Why do we have to make anything? How about we order it?" I suggested.

"No, that costs more money, even if we burn some cookies it doesn't cost as much."

I nodded. "Maybe, I can buy it, since I ruined it," I offered, holding my breath.

He moved and kissed my cheek, "don't worry, I got it, maybe you can help Ryan fix lighting in the back."

I looked at Ryan outside, standing on the ladder. The last time I spoke to him, I had called him a convict.

"I think he got it covered, doesn't look like he needs help," I shrugged and Xander sniggered.

"Okay, then you can just stand there and look pretty. I can't say I mind the view," he winked while he mixed sugar and cream for the frosting.

"Fine, I'll go help Ryan."

I offered to help Ryan, but he basically just told me to hand him the lights and clippers while he did all the work standing on that ladder. One of the kids could have helped him with lights and clippers.

After a long silence between us, Ryan said, "Glad that you are making an effort for Xander, he really likes you."

"Thanks for the insight," I remarked, handing him another light.

He laughed.

"I'm surprised Xander forgave you after that stunt you pulled, bringing in Simon."

I froze in place and then met his eyes, "Ryan? Is it? Or should I call you the cheater ex?" I watched him fume and took satisfaction in it.

"Xander is..." he started to say, but I interrupted.

"I would have loved to stay and chit chat about what went down between Xander and me if I thought your opinion was worth considering," I started to leave when he said.

"Hey man, it's Christmas. Lets not fight. Xander and I grew up together in this same house. I always looked out for him. I will always care about him. He is family, but we were not meant to be together. We were too young and stupid. He deserved so much better than a cheating boyfriend, and I am glad he found you."

"Thank you," I was surprised at his admission.

He smiled and gave me a big hug, "Welcome to the family." He said, which surprised me more.

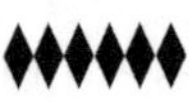

I watched Xander, Ryan, and Mrs. Cook working in the kitchen. Most big kids were cleaning the house and decorating, while I helped young kids wrap some presents.

"That's glue. It's not frosting," I grabbed the glue from one of the kids and hid it.

"I want glitter," the kid protested.

"You have enough glitter on your face already."

"No, I want more," he tried to get the glitter box and slipped, making the whole box fly in the air only to land right back on top of me. They all laughed at my predicament.

"Glad you enjoyed the show," I said, clearing glitter out of my hair.

"Now, you have glitter on your face," the kid remarked.

"I am aware of it." I said cleaning my face. "Now, clean up. The glitter goes back in the box," I ordered and kids got to work.

These kids were making presents for each other, playing a Santa. Mrs. Cook said that she wanted these kids to know that they had to look out for each other, because there was no Santa. They had to be the Santa for each other. I thought it was sweet. Growing up, I didn't care much for Santa, my sister was the one who made a personalized gift for me, and finding that one gift out of so many was the highlight of my Christmas.

"Myles," Xander came and sat beside me while I was busy snatching the glue from another kid which sputtered all over my shirt, making those glitters permanent.

"I am going to sue you," I threatened the kid.

Xander laughed. "You look pretty," he said, cleaning glitter off me. "I think glitter is your thing."

"Haha," I sneered.

"Myles, it's sweet of you to help but you don't have to stay, if you have to go to your parents' for Christmas," he ran his fingers through my hair to clean off glitter and it felt nice.

"My parents are in Paris like every year and since Sophie got married, we barely celebrate Christmas together. So, I'd like to stay here, if that's okay?"

Xander smiled and kissed my cheek, "I love you," he said.

"I love you, too." I moved forward to kiss him but one kid interrupted with his wrapped toy in my face. He wanted a ribbon for his toy.

Xander laughed, grabbed the gift and placed a flower ribbon around it.

We then decorated the gifts under the tree and Ryan switched on the lights. Everything looked beautiful. The lights didn't have the professional touch that I was used to seeing, but it was just perfect, like this is how it was supposed to be. I wrapped my arm around Xander as we admired the lights around the house.

"This is perfect," I expressed.

"It's perfect with you," Xander hugged me "I am so happy you came." his warm breath fell on my ear, making me desperate for him.

"Me too," I held him tight.

After that, we had dinner and cookies, which I didn't know could taste so good with turkey. Everything was perfect and it felt like home, a home I didn't know I never had.

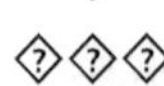

Next Book in the series:
If I Didn't Know Better...
M/M Second Chance Romance
The Right One Series.

You may access *If I Didn't Know Better...* **the next phase in the lives of Myles and Xander, along with Preston and Ryan.**

To learn about new releases from A.B Julian. Please visit A.B Julian's website for some free stories: https://abjulian.com